ICE PRINCESS

EMBER-RAINE WINTERS

CONTENTS

PROLOGUE

Before the fall of the Kingdoms, centuries of peace reigned between the four kingdoms. Their subjects lived good and prosperous lives. But not all beings wanted peace and weaved derision amongst the people and the four Queens. Something dark lurked within the Kingdoms that not even the most powerful seers could fathom. The all-powerful Queens had seers, the most powerful beings in the realms, as advisors. It is told that before the eternal darkness came, each Queen's seer had a vision of the world being thrown into chaos. When this happens, the young princesses would not survive if they stayed in their Kingdoms. They were sent away for their safety so that once they came of age, they could bring back the light into the darkness as the prophecy foretold.

Only the Queens and their most trusted advisors knew

about the princesses and their role in the prophecy. When the Dark Fae attacked, they razed the Kingdoms in search of the girls and brought about the endless darkness the seers had predicted. The Queens longed for their daughters but delighted in the fact that the dark demons wouldn't find the girls. Once the princesses were powerful enough to bring back the light, they would return. The Queens hoped by the time the girls came into their power it wouldn't be too late to save the realm of Avalon. If Avalon falls, all the realms fall with it.

1

FREESIA

"Freesia? What are you doing outside? The wind is freezing. You know mother doesn't like when you wonder off in the cold." That was my adopted sister, Molly. She was always trying to keep me out of trouble, even though she was three years younger and I was practically an adult. I smiled at her.

"I don't feel the cold, Molly. You know that." I ruffled her hair as she scowled. I could tell she was already too cold to be outside. I never understood why my family lived in the frozen tundra. They couldn't handle the temperature the way I could. My father was better about it. He could go out without much problems.

"You're so weird." She snuggled into me for warmth. She only did that when we were outside and she was cold.

"Go inside, Moll. I'm going to watch the flurries for a bit.

I promise I won't go far." I raised an eyebrow at her.

"Mom won't like it. She said there are dark things out there." She peered into the trees as if she expected something to jump from the shadows at any moment.

"Boo," I cackled as she shrieked, jumping about a foot in the air and clinging to me for a second before her fist slammed into my arm hard.

"You're so mean," she wailed. "You scared me. It isn't funny." I couldn't help but continue the roar of laughter that burst forth. My annoying little sister was so skittish it was ridiculous. All the tactics mother and father tried to use on me to get me to fear the outside world only fed my curiosity. But poor Molls became more skittish and scared of her own shadow by the day.

"Freesia, please don't scare Molly. She's… delicate." Athos, my father shot me a stern glare, and I nodded before bowing my head.

"Sorry, Molls," I got the words out before she whirled on our father.

"I am not delicate." She stomped her foot as she glared at him. I coughed, trying to hide my giggle. She wanted to be tough, but it was hard when she was scared of her own shadow most of the time. Her thick mahogany hair was such a contrast to my pale blonde strands. I sometimes wondered about my real family because I was the opposite from my parents and sister in every way. My eyes were a clear crystal shade of blue that looked like ice. Molly had dark brown eyes the color of melted chocolate. Their skin was pale but not porcelain like mine. They probably would have been a rich tan color if they hadn't spent the last seventeen years living in the tundra. Athos never told me about where they lived before they adopted me, but I was sure it was some place exotic and warm.

"Freesia, you know your mother doesn't like you wandering around in the cold," Athos grumbled. I knew they were just trying to protect us, but it grated on me. Mother was always telling crazy stories about dark creatures just to scare us and Athos just let her keep me caged. I hated it.

"I just wanted to play in the snow, father," I pouted. His eyes softened for a second, but he shook his head.

"Come on, let's go into the training room and get some of that pent up energy out of you." He grinned, but it didn't reach his eyes. He didn't like keeping me cooped up any more than I did, but if mother found out he'd let me stay out in the snow, there would be hell to pay. I grumbled under my breath as I stomped into the house, which was more like a giant stone fortress. It was beautiful, but a beautiful cage was still a cage.

As I made my way through the main hall, Baskin, one of the many guards we had in the house sidled up to me. "Trying to escape again, princess?" He smiled mischievously, and I glared at him.

"Stop calling me that," I groaned.

"Why?" He looked puzzled. Baskin was about my age, with dark blond hair and eyes the color I imagined the ocean to the south would look like. I longed to see it for myself, to feel the massive power of the crashing waves, but that wasn't possible for me. I was stuck in the frozen tundra to keep me *safe.* I had no idea what was so dangerous. Anytime I brought it up, the conversation would end and everyone involved would shut down completely.

"I don't like it. I don't want to be a princess locked away in a gilded cage. I want to be out there exploring the world. So stop with the princess jokes." Baskin's face fell slightly and guilt washed over me. I hadn't meant to be mean to him, I was just angry at the whole situation. I couldn't even go outside and play in the snow. It was ridiculous.

We walked into the training room. It was a big stone hall about a hundred feet long and had every kind of weapon on the walls. There were cabinets lining the space to hold the smaller weapons and arrows for the beautiful bows that were displayed. Two wooden targets sat at the end of the hall off to the side of the sparring platform. They kept the two as separate as possible so the guards could spar and work on shooting at the same time. I picked up my beautiful silver bow. It was intricately carved to look like it had ice crystals and snowflakes all over the handle. It buzzed in my hand as it always did. It felt strange but comforting, like the bow was alive and happy to see me when I touched it. I shrugged and pulled my arrows from the drawer. No one else used my weapons, they were always there waiting for me. It was odd, but I didn't really think much on it. I slung the quiver over my shoulder and got into position. The bow still buzzed in my hand as I knocked my first arrow got into position and cleared my mind before I let it fly.

I watched as it sailed through the air and went directly into the center of the target. Baskin let out a whoop as I grinned. I continued for hours, letting all my anger and frustrations out on the targets until my arm was sore and I could barely hold up the bow anymore. "You shouldn't work so hard. You're going to hurt yourself." Baskin eyed me warily.

"I'm fine," I grumbled as I put my stuff away and headed to the dining room. I was going to eat, then hide in my room for the rest of the night. Away from everyone. I'd rather be alone in my room than around the people who decided I wasn't even allowed to go outside. It was torture.

I ate quickly and made polite conversation before I excused myself and headed up the marble staircase to my rooms. Sighing, I closed the door, locking it behind me as I made my way to the balcony and opened the door. I breathed in deeply of the crisp winter air. I loved being outside. I wished they could all see what they were doing to me by keeping me in my pretty cage.

I watched the snow flurries dance and grinned as I held out my hand and they danced on my palm. They swirled in a tiny vortex and I wiggled my fingers, causing them to jump and dance some more. I'd learned I could control the snow a few years back, but it was something I kept to myself. Father and mother would not like the power I had and I wouldn't even be able to step out onto the balcony anymore. It was my private space, but even here I had a guard at the bottom of the stairs who would stop me from leaving the security of the compound.

A low-pitched whine startled me from my thoughts and I looked toward the shadows at the far end of the balcony. Piercing gray eyes met mine as the animal whined again. I stepped cautiously, not wanting to spook it and it watched me intently. It whined again as I drew closer, holding out my hand to show I meant it no harm.

"Shhh, it's okay. I'm not going to hurt you. How did you get up here?" My eyes adjusted to the shadows, and I finally saw the animal for the first time. It was a beautiful wolf as white as the purest snow, except its front paw was streaked with red where it lay injured on my balcony. "Can I help you with that?" I pointed at the bloody paw and the beautiful animal whimpered again. I looked at the gashes and grimaced. It looked like it had gotten caught in some kind of trap. Were they out at night trapping animals for sport? I was going to have a serious talk with my father about that in the morning, but first I needed to help the injured wolf.

"Freesia?" the night guard Alec called up the stairs. "Is there someone there with you?" It sounded like he was about to climb the stairs. I couldn't let him find the injured wolf. There was no telling what he might do with it.

"No, I'm talking to myself, you know because I'm locked in my cage alone and crazy," I snarked and heard him grumble as he stepped back down the steps. "Stay there I'm going to help you," I whispered to the wolf before rushing inside, hoping it didn't leave while Alec was right there and already suspicious.

2

WESTON

I shouldn't have gone that far south. I knew it was dangerous and I was putting the entire pack at risk, but I couldn't bring myself to care as I sat there injured and waiting for the beauty to come back. She was entrancing, with hair that shown like the moon and clear blue eyes that looked to be cut from the most beautiful diamonds. I didn't want to move and I couldn't have even if I'd wanted to. It had been hard enough getting up the stairs after that bear trap ensnared my paw. I'd had to shift partially just to get out, and that had been excruciating in my current state. I'd had no idea what else to do. All I knew was I needed to get out of the elements and rest so I could heal myself. I hadn't expected anyone to walk out on the balcony in the freezing temps and start playing with the snowflakes.

I'd watched as they'd danced for her. Her inner glow had

shone like a beacon. I guessed she had no idea what she was. I did, though. I was betting she was the lost Ice Princess from a world that was no longer ours. She came back quickly with a bowl of warm water and a washcloth and started dabbing at my wound. My wolf whimpered at the pain, but she rubbed her free hand over the silky fur on my side.

"I'm sorry, I'm not trying to hurt you," she whispered so that the guard at the bottom of the stairs wouldn't hear. I wondered what he was doing there. Was she a prisoner? My wolf growled low at the thought which made the girl jump back startled. Shit. I needed to curb my thoughts, or the wolf would scare her away. I bumped her hand with my snout and nuzzled her palm. Closing my eyes, I felt something I'd never felt in all my centuries of life. A connection so strong I couldn't even describe it. My wolf wanted to howl, but I held tight to my control. We couldn't let her know what we were yet and definitely couldn't tell her what she was to us. My wolf snarled in my head. He was all instinct and I knew what he wanted, but I held him back. This girl was ignorant of our world. Whoever had stolen her away from her home had made sure of it. I almost growled again, but managed to hold back.

My pack had served the Ice Queen for centuries. We were her most trusted warriors, and even we weren't aware that the princess had gone missing until it was too late. The Dark Fae came like thieves in the night and destroyed our homeland, filling it with darkness and pain. All who could, fled to this world until we could find the stolen princesses and restore the four Kingdoms. And the whole time the Ice Princess had been mere miles away from the safety of the pack, hidden away in a fortress, wasting away without any knowledge of her home or her magic.

I almost growled again as I watched her concentrate as she cleaned my wounds. Her brows scrunched together as she worked to clean the blood and wrap my paw. Every touch was like magic. I couldn't get enough of her clear blue eyes. It's the only reason I let her waste her time on a wound that would heal easily by morning. She thought I was a wild animal, and still she showed compassion and little fear in the face of my giant wolf.

I nudged her hand with my head again, licking her fingers and nearly groaned. She giggled as she pulled her hand away and scratched at my ears. My tongue lolled out of my mouth as I felt her fingers run through my silky fur. I had no idea what this girl was doing to me. I was a fierce protector and warrior, not a fucking lap dog.

"Let's get you inside where it's warm." She patted my head and I couldn't help but lean into the touch. I was so done for. The pack would have my hide for putting them in danger by coming here, but I couldn't take my eyes off the princess as she led me inside the warm room and shut the doors to the balcony and locked them.

I would have to shift to get out of here, and that would definitely alert the guard at the steps to my presence. Shit. How was I going to get myself out of this mess? It wasn't like I could stay there. Someone was bound to come in and wonder why the princess had a wolf in her room. I was so fucked.

She ran her fingers down my back, and I shuddered at the soft caress. If only she knew what she was doing to me. My wolf snarled in my head. *Mate.* Yeah, well, at least we were on the same page about that, but there was no way I could act on it. There was a knock on the door and a gruff male voice called from the other side. "Freesia, open the door. We need to talk." I recognized the voice immediately. It had been seventeen years since I'd heard it, but it still sounded the same. *Athos.* He had been the Queen's most trusted advisor before the war when he disappeared without a trace. Many thought he'd gone to the dark while others just thought him a coward, but no one had seen him since.

Nothing made sense as I padded into Freesia's bathroom and laid in the tub. She looked at me strangely before closing the door until it was only open a crack. With my superior hearing, I listened from my spot in the tub trying to figure out what the hell was going on here. I heard the door click open and the stomping of boots as he strolled into the room, probably searching for anything amiss. "What do you want, father?" I could hear the censure in her tone. Wait? Father? That man wasn't her father. He was her abductor. What had the man done to brainwash the poor princess? I nearly growled, but that would have given me away and this situation had just become exceedingly more dangerous. Athos would recognize me for what I was and kill me if he thought I was a threat to whatever plan he had for her.

"I want you to stop stomping around the compound like a spoiled child who didn't get her way. You have no idea the sacrifices we have all made to be here to keep you safe," he yelled. Her breath caught, and I wanted to jump out of the tub and challenge him. No one had the right to speak to her like that. She was our Queen. Or, she would be if I had anything to say about it. "We have all given up our lives and homes to protect you, and all you do is complain and throw fits about not being allowed outside the walls. I have had enough. You will stay in your room until you can learn to be grateful to the people who work around the clock to make sure nothing bad happens to you."

"Maybe if you actually told me what was out there instead of letting mother yell insane bedtime stories meant to scare me into obedience, then I would be more prepared for what is out there." I heard the balcony door crash open and a howling gust of wind whooshed through the room.

Easing out of the tub, I watched as it swirled around the princess in a protective shield. Athos' jaw dropped as he backed away from Freesia. Hair the color of moonlight whipped around her head as she glared at Athos. "You need to trust that I can handle myself," her voice was deadly calm as the wind circled around her, picking her up off her feet. If Athos didn't do something, she was going to let the wind whisk her away to the forest where there were bear traps and Dark Fae still hunting for the stolen princesses.

"Freesia, you need to calm down. I can't explain anything to you yet, but as soon as I can I will. Please. Don't do this. Don't let the wind take you off into the unknown. It's not safe."

"Ugh, you think I can't take care of myself? You have been training me in survival from the time I could walk. You know I'm more than capable." She crossed her arms over her chest as the wind continued to pick up speed. Athos' eyes glinted dangerously as his head cocked in my direction. Shit. With the wind she was channeling, I was downwind of the advisor and it looked as if he had picked up my scent.

"Who's here with you?" he growled and started to walk to the bathroom. *Shit. I was a goner.*

"No one. I found a wounded animal on the balcony and it needed my help. I knew you wouldn't approve, so I put it in the bathroom." Well, that wasn't exactly the way it had gone, but I shrugged.

"Weston of the snow wolf pack show yourself," Athos roared. I padded out in my wolf form with my head held high and snarled at Athos as I placed myself in front of my mate. Shit. I couldn't think of her like that.

"What is this? You know a pack of wolves?" Freesia was cute when she was confused.

"He isn't just a normal wolf. He's a shifter, and that superficial wound you treated will heal by morning," Athos chuckled and I snarled at him again. "Shift," he barked at me before telling Freesia to turn around. We both complied, and he grabbed a throw blanket off the couch next to her bed and threw it to me. I quickly wrapped it around my waist.

"Athos. How could you betray your Queen? You were her favorite, and you repaid her by abducting her only child? To what ends? To keep her locked in an ivory tower, never to fulfill her destiny? Because of you our world is dead, as is our Queen and all the other monarchs." I had no idea at what point I had moved to get in his face, but we were practically nose to nose.

"You have no idea what you're talking about, mutt. We gave up our entire lives and our realm to keep her safe."

"Easy for you to say now that the Queen isn't here to refute your claims," I growled.

"Wait, what's going on? What are you talking about?" Freesia cried from behind me. "You're the wolf?" She stumbled, and I caught her just as she fainted from the shock.

Athos attempted to take her from me, and I snarled and snapped at him. "Mine."

"You can't be serious." He threw his hands up in the air. "How in the living fuck did that happen?"

My arms tightened around her as I held her body against me. I didn't want him touching her. My wolf was so close to the surface that Athos took a step back. "I knew the minute she touched me to bandage my paw. Even if it was pointless, I couldn't tell her no." I sighed. "Look, I didn't come here looking for trouble. I got caught in a trap not far from here and the storm was getting bad. Her balcony was the only shelter for miles. I didn't think anyone would come outside in the middle of a storm to play with snowflakes." I shook my head as I smiled down at the beautiful princess in my arms.

"What do you mean playing with snowflakes? She did magic?" His face turned white as a sheet as he looked around the room, as if something was going to jump out to grab her at any second. Over my dead body. I snarled.

"Yes, why do you look like a ghoul?" I raised a brow at him. What the hell was going on?

"The Queen bound her powers herself to keep her hidden until it was time to take her place within the four Kingdoms. It's too soon. She's not ready to take on the darkness. The other princesses are still hidden. She can't be the first to awaken. She can't. Shit." I'd never known the warrior babble like that. I held the princess closer until she started to squirm, and I had to reluctantly let her go. I hoped it wouldn't be the only time I ever got to hold her like that. It would end me if it was.

3

FREESIA

My eyes snapped open. I was snuggled against a warm chest. What had father called him? Weston? I struggled to get out of his arms, even though it was the last thing I wanted to do. Maybe I was crazy, or this was some bizarre dream. I didn't think so. It felt way too real to be a hallucination or a dream.

"Have you been using magic?" father's tone was accusatory, and I spun around to glare at him.

"What do you know about magic?" I barked back at him.

"I know we went to great lengths to keep you from using it before it was time for you to take your rightful place as Queen." He glared at me.

"What do you mean, Queen? I'm no Queen. Has everyone lost their minds?" I threw my hands up in the air. A hand came down on my shoulder, and a soothing feeling ran through me.

I had no idea what it was, or why Weston's touch had that effect on me, but I instinctively knew it was him. I swayed a little on my feet and his other hand moved to my waist to steady me. I heard a low growl and lifted an eyebrow at Athos.

"Keep your hands to yourself, pup," he grumbled.

"You know I'm no pup," his voice was silky smooth where it sounded from behind me, and I found myself leaning back to soak up his warmth. What was I doing? I didn't even know this person or shifter or whatever the hell he was. But for some strange reason, I felt drawn to him. His black hair was such a contrast to the silky white fur of his wolf, but his eyes, they were the exact shade of steel gray and seemed to glow in the dim light of the bedroom. I would've gotten lost in them, if father hadn't cleared his throat.

"Hold on a second. Did you kidnap me from my home?" I had to be sure. "Who is my real father?"

"I don't know," he sighed. "The Queen had many consorts, and there is no way to know which of us is your true father." He looked away at the word "us."

"You were one of them?" Jeez, was that really what I wanted to know, that my mother, the all-powerful Ice Queen, had been a promiscuous slutbag? What was wrong with me? I swayed on my feet again and felt warm hands on my hips steadying me.

"I was. It is possible I am your true father, but you look more like another." He shrugged. The idea that there was someone else who looked similar to me made me shake my head. This man had raised me, and even though he had been part of the group that sought to cage me, I still thought of him as my father. A shout from down the hall had the three of us turning our heads. Baskin launched himself into the room, throwing my bow at me, and I caught it in one hand. "Report."

"Bears, sir. They are trying to get passed the perimeter." He breathed heavily.

"Are you friends with bears?" I looked over my shoulder at Weston, who shook his head.

"Once the Kingdoms fell, the bears gave their allegiance to the Dark Fae, along with the night wolf pack and a few other undesirables. The Snow Wolves and most of the big cats fled to this realm in search of the lost princesses and a way to rid our world from their evil." Father nodded like he had heard that information before. I was sure he had. "You have been keeping in touch with someone from home?" Weston raised a brow in accusation.

"There are spies in the dark castle, yes."

"Hello? Bears are surrounding the compound," Baskin yelled, and threw his hands in the air.

"You know the drill, sound the alarms. I don't care how many you kill as long as you take one alive for questioning," Athos yelled, and Baskin ran off.

I screamed as the wood and glass of the balcony doors shattered as Alec was thrown through them. He landed in a bloody heap on the ground in front of us. One second I was on my feet and the next I was lying on the soft rug with a very hard body on top of mine. Weston's gray eyes glinted in the candlelit room and I could see the wolf looking through them.

"Don't worry. I'll keep you safe. Stay here, don't let them see you." He winked before jumping up and landing in front of the doors in his wolf form. I moved to the bed with my bow at the ready, but Weston was jumping and snarling at the giant Kodiak and I couldn't get a clear shot.

The great white wolf snapped his jaw onto the bear's femur and it stood on its hind legs with a roar, finally giving me the perfect opportunity to shoot it. I let the arrow fly, and it pierced the left side of the beast's chest. I hated that I'd had to kill the beast, but even as it was falling it took one last swipe at Weston throwing him into a wall like a rag doll. I gasped as I lunged for Weston, only to have strong arms hold me back.

"You stay hidden and make sure your bow is at the ready. I'll check on the mutt." Father grinned.

"Stop calling him that," I mumbled, too numb to argue. I needed to watch for more bears. A glowing light emitted from the bear's chest as it slowly shifted back to its humanoid shape, only this was unlike any other human I'd ever seen. He had a deep tan and jet black hair. His eyes were wide in death, but I could see where black lines crisscrossed through his veins, covering his entire body like his blood had turned black with his evil intentions. It made me shudder with revulsion, and I no longer cared about killing the vile thing.

A roar sounded in the distance and I flinched. I wondered how many more there were out there. I shivered as I watched the man with the black veins shimmer before turning to dust on my floor.

A second later, Baskin was in the doorway looking like

he'd been mauled. "They are retreating, sir," he said to my father, who was leaning over Weston.

"Fortify everything and double the traps. We will have to leave here soon, signal everyone to pack the essentials. We leave at daybreak when they are least likely to attack." He fired off the orders and Baskin left the room. We were leaving? We'd never even been outside the compound. "I guess you get your wish, princess. So how does it feel?" Father asked me, and I flinched at his snide tone.

"Leave her alone," Weston huffed. "You kept her in the dark, it's only normal for her to want a glimpse of the things she's been forbidden to see her whole life." He glared at my father.

"We have to leave our home because they found us. They probably followed the scent of your blood through the forest, so don't go telling me how to talk to the girl *I* have raised from an infant." Father jumped off the ground and stalked toward me. "I hope you're happy. You're finally getting what you want, but at what cost? Hmmm. The potential loss of everyone who has already given up everything to keep you safe." He stormed from the room and I fell to the ground, curling into a ball, and letting my sobs take me. It was my fault they were there, and it was my fault they had to leave. Maybe, just maybe, if I wasn't there, they wouldn't have to sacrifice their home and safety. The bears would leave them alone if I was gone.

I let the tears dry and jumped up to grab my satchel and fill it with the things I might need. Weston was next to me in a second, halting my hand. "What are you doing?" he asked softly. Letting a breath out, I looked into his steel-gray eyes.

"I'm leaving. Maybe they won't have to sacrifice everything for me again if I'm not here. The bears will come after me and leave them in peace. I don't need protection, I killed that bear on my own. I don't need their sacrifices." The stubborn wolf turned me around to face him. I was acutely aware of the fact that he still wasn't wearing anything except for the throw blanket that had been on my couch. His tan skin made my mouth water, and I sucked in a breath.

"Are you sure you want to do this?" He lifted my chin, so I wasn't looking at his impressive chest. "These people care about you. They want you safe no matter what."

"Did you hear the way father just blamed me for them all having to sacrifice for me again? I can't take everyone blaming me because I was unhappy being treated like a prisoner. If they are happy here, I don't want them to give up their lives for me again. I'm leaving before they can." I huffed and turned to leave off the balcony. Weston groaned and followed.

"Well, if you're going to go out there. You aren't going alone. I'll go with you." I looked at him dubiously because he still wasn't wearing any clothes. He chuckled, and the sound set my nerves on fire. "I'm a much better protector in my wolf form, but if you want a companion, I left some clothes about two miles north of here."

"Are you sure? I can do this on my own. I don't want anyone else to sacrifice their life for mine." The way father had said sacrifice like I owed my entire existence to them made my stomach plummet. I never asked them to do it. And if my real mother had, then that was on her, not me. She owed them a debt that she would never be able to repay. I know I sounded like a spoiled brat, but I hadn't asked to be the last hope for the Kingdoms, a place I didn't even remember and I didn't ask Mother and father to sacrifice their every happiness to keep me safe and protected. I didn't want safe. I wanted adventure and freedom, things I'd never experienced from my pretty cage.

"Well then, let's go." He grinned, shifting into his wolf and nudging me to get on his back. My face screwed up like he was crazy and he yipped before nudging me again.

"Isn't this dehumanizing?" I raised a brow, and the wolf rolled his eyes before nudging me again. I giggled. "Okay, I get the point. You want me to ride on your back." He nodded and lowered himself so it was easier for me. Standing upright in his wolf form, he came up to my chest in height. I climbed on and slid my fingers through the soft fur at his neck, and I could have sworn he purred.

Hold on tight. His voice sounded like silk in my head.

"You can read my mind?" I asked out loud.

No, but when I'm in this form, I can talk to you telepathically. Try it. I didn't know what he thought I could do, but I tried saying something mundane.

Hi. He nodded his head.

Very good. Now we don't have to give away our location by speaking out loud. You ready to go? I looked around my room. I had everything I could need, including my bow and quiver slung over my shoulder, but the thought of leaving made me sad for some reason. I strengthened my resolve and nodded before finding the telepathic link between Weston and me.

Yes, I'm ready. Let's go, I said into his mind and he took off faster than I could have thought possible. I didn't hesitate as I went with Weston. There was a shout in the distance, and I leaned over Weston's back, trying to make myself blend into his silky white coat. I could almost do it with my ultra pale features. The shouting grew louder, and I urged him to go faster with my mind. I didn't want them to find us. Maybe if I was gone, they could go back to their old lives.

There is no going back, Weston said into my head.

I thought you said you couldn't read my thoughts? I lifted a brow, but he couldn't see it with me riding on his back.

You were practically screaming in my head. If you want your thoughts kept private, maybe stop holding on so tight to the mental link. I growled angrily. I wasn't trying to shout my thoughts at him, and he knew that I knew very little about our world and magic and shifters. *I'm sorry but the faster you realize that taking you saved them untold loss, the happier you will be. They made you feel guilty for their sacrifices they made for you, but if they haven't made those sacrifices, they wouldn't have lived long enough to feel the weight of their own decisions. They made the decision to steal you away for your own protection and for them to be angry that you didn't under-stand is just unfair.* He leaned his head back and licked my nose, causing me to giggle. *Now stop distracting me with your cute little nose in my fur. We need to get out of here.* I took a deep inhale and noticed how he smelled like the first snowfall of winter and freshly fallen pine needles. He groaned inside my head, causing me to smile. He felt it too, this connection between us that was super weird considering I thought he was just an animal at first. It was unlike anything I'd ever felt before. I wasn't sure I wanted to feel it with anyone else either, which was even weirder.

4

———————

WESTON

I ran through the forest faster than ever before. I could smell the bears everywhere. It made me antsy knowing they were out there looking for the princess. The only solace I had was the fact that I was faster than them by a long shot. I could get her to the safety of the pack before the bears could even pick up her scent. There were wards around the pack's lands. Nothing dark could get within a ten-mile radius without us knowing. Freesia would be safe, but I knew she wouldn't want to be cooped up again. At least she would be able to go outside as long as she didn't wander too far. Was I caging her again the same way Athos had done by taking her to pack lands? I hoped she wouldn't see it that way.

A couple miles away from the compound, I slowed just long enough to grab my pack, then kept going. The sooner we got away from the threat of the bears, the sooner she would be

safe. In all my five hundred years, I had never wanted something so bad as I wanted to keep her safe happy. Even though
the two wants contradicted each other. I wanted her to be free,
but I also needed her to be safe. Maybe there was a way for
her to have both. If we could find the other princesses and
destroy the dark, she could have everything she ever wanted.
The thought seemed impossible. Who knew what realms the
other princesses were in.

*We are almost to the pack's lands. You'll be safe there until
we figure out what to do next,* I said directly into her mind.
She sighed as she nodded into my fur. Having her close to me
like that made the mate bond solidify even more. I could feel it
snapping into place. She scratched her nails into my fur, and I
couldn't help the feral groan that escaped. She had no idea
what she was doing to me, and I couldn't stop to explain how
wolves viewed touch, especially among mates. I couldn't tell
her about the mate bond we had. It was too soon, and she had
no idea what was happening between us. She didn't even truly
understand what she was.

It wasn't too long after that when I felt her fall asleep on
my back and slowed my pace just a little. I didn't want her
falling off. She was so exhausted from the events of the day.
We were almost to the edge of the wards. It wouldn't be long
now before we were in the safety of the pack's lands. I
wondered what the elders would say. They had no jurisdiction
over me since I wasn't technically one of theirs. I was an
anomaly. I didn't really belong anywhere, but the Snow
Wolves' pack had taken me in and made me one of their own.

Don't fall off, precious, I said into her mind and felt her stir a little. I noticed she didn't like the title of princess, even though that was exactly what she was. *We are almost to the pack's lands and we will decide what to do once we get there.* She nodded into my fur before she straightened. I could feel her reluctance at going into the unknown. She had no reason to trust that the pack wouldn't trap her like her own family had. The only person she would know is me, and we didn't really know each other either. I would die, though, before I let them chain her.

We *will decide what to do next. The pack has no control over me. And they definitely don't control you. They are only a resting ground before we decide what to do next.* I reached my head back and I couldn't stop the wolf from licking her face. She tasted like the first pure snow of the year. She smiled shyly at me and the wolf yipped. I grinned on the inside, knowing she could feel it too.

Right on the outside of the pack's lands, I smelled something that shouldn't have been there. The pack never left the safety of their wards, and it made my hackles rise. These weren't wolves from the Snow Wolves pack. *I need you to stay as close to my back as you can, precious. There are wolves I don't know surrounding the wards,* I said into her mind. She stiffened and buried her face in my neck. I couldn't enjoy the sensation over the sheer terror pulsing through me. Had the dark wolves found us? Was it all my fault? Shit. I never should have ventured that far. If I hadn't though, what would have happened to Freesia? Would the bears have gotten their filthy paws on her? There was no time to think about what ifs. I needed to think of a plan to get passed the wolves and behind the safety of the wards. I padded on silent feet to get as close to the wards as I could without being seen, but there was nothing I could do to hide our smell. I was a hundred feet from the wards when I heard the first growl. *Do you still have that pretty bow?* I asked her telepathically, and she nodded into my fur. *Can you shoot from your position on my back without making yourself a target?* The last thing I wanted her to do was sit up and make it so much easier for her to be taken down.

I might need to sit up. I've never shot a bow of the back of a wolf before. She giggled inside my head. I grinned to myself, even though this definitely wasn't the time or place for laughter. We were being stalked by a pack of evil shifters hell bent on stealing the princess. The wolves weren't even trying to be stealthy. They were fucking with us. They wanted us to know that we were surrounded.

Hold on tight with your thighs and knock an arrow. I won't let you fall, but you need to keep your balance as best as you can. It's going to be a fight to get out of here.

I felt her nod against me as she shifted, her thighs squeezed against my flank, and I almost changed my mind about the position we were in. I was thinking all kinds of inappropriate thoughts that had no place in our current predicament. She shifted again, and I could tell she was knocking an arrow, ready and waiting for my signal. I still couldn't see the wolves, but I could feel their presence. They were waiting for something. I didn't want to wait around to see what that could be, so I charged the wolf closest to the wards and shouted at Freesia with my mind to open fire. The wolf dodged, but somehow the princess anticipated its move and the arrow sunk into the wolf's side. It yelped as it fell to the ground and I jumped over it just as another one came barreling toward us from the side. The princess knocked another arrow, hitting the wolf in the chest before it could get close, but two more were gaining ground. They were trying to split our attention by attacking from both sides.

Suddenly Freesia sat up and clapped her hands together. I wanted to yell at her to get down, but just at that second ice spears formed on the trees above the wolves and fell, impaling each of the creatures. Dark blood splattered onto both of us, but I didn't stop to examine the scene. I leapt through the ward just as a bear swiped its paw at me and bellowed in frustration. I felt pain in my back flank but didn't stop until we were far enough into the pack's lands that the bears and wolves couldn't sense us.

Finally, I collapsed on the ground with a thud and a yelp. The bear had got me. I tried not to show how much pain I was in, but after running for miles with claw marks in my leg, it was near impossible. Freesia hopped off my back and gave me a concerned look as she stepped to the side to look at the open wound on my leg.

"The only thing I have to clean it with is snow." Her forehead creased in concentration. My wolf whined. He wanted to move to protect her, but he couldn't, and we were both feeling frustrated.

"The snow will help numb the pain as well. Do you think you will be able to shift? Will that help with healing? It seemed to help with your paw earlier." She was rambling, and it was fucking adorable.

Pack some snow on there and we will see how it goes. If it's numb, I should be able to shift and heal myself. I braced myself for the sizzling pain that would come from the ice touching my heated skin. It would hurt at first, but I could already feel my body trying to heal. The snow was a balm instead of the fiery agony I'd expected. I relaxed beneath Freesia's soothing touch as she cleaned and packed more soft snow into the open wounds.

"Is that better?" she asked hesitantly. I nodded my head, and she breathed a sigh of relief. "Good. I'm glad. Can you shift?" She kept looking around, clutching her bow over her shoulder as if she expected the dark wolves and bears to show up at any time. I nuzzled her hand with my nose.

We are inside pack lands now, those other shifters can't get passed the wards. Her hand came up to scratch behind my ears and my wolf practically purred like a damn cat. What the fuck we don't purr. The wolf licked her hand, and I groaned. He was way too content with her. Way too attached already. What if she didn't feel the bond the same way we did? It could turn on us. I couldn't let the wolf get attached so quickly, only to have her choose another. We wouldn't be able to handle it, and no one wanted to see us go rogue. I decided to end their connection and shifted, giving Freesia a subtle warning to move back. She did as I instructed as the light washed over me and I returned to my human form. Her eyes widened and her cheeks flushed as she turned away to let me get dressed. I'd only seen it for a second, but I could have sworn there was desire in her eyes as she'd looked at me. I grinned.

"You can turn around now, precious," I said after I was fully clothed. She peeked at me from the corner of her eye, not trusting that I was fully dressed. Her cheeks were still pink as she faced me fully.

"What do we do now?" She rung her hands together.

"The pack elders will know what to do. They may even know where to go next. Do you need to rest? It's only a couple miles to the pack compound." I rubbed her arm soothingly. I wondered if she could feel the cold and if I should risk wrapping my arm around her to warm her up. Maybe it was just my need to be so close. She was the Ice Princess, the only heir to the Ice Queen's thrown. She probably didn't feel the cold. I wrapped my arm around her anyway, and she snuggled against me.

"Let's just keep moving. I don't like being in the open like this with those things out there searching for us." She shuddered. I wanted to remind her that the wards would keep them out, but it seemed like a waste of breath as she snuggled into me.

"Are you cold?" I asked as I squeezed her closer to me.

"No, I don't feel cold. I'm a little scared though. Maybe I

never should have left. Maybe I should have let them move me and continue to cage me for my own protection."

"If you would have stayed, every one of them would have been in danger. They never would have smelled the wolves the way I did. They would have been ambushed and you would have been taken to Gods know where. Don't ever doubt your instincts." I tilted her chin up so I could look into her ice-blue eyes. "You did the right thing, Freesia. We will make sure your people are safe." And just because I'm an instinctual asshole, I kissed her on the cheek. My wolf growled in approval as her eyes fluttered closed.

5

FREESIA

My heart warmed at the gentle press of his lips to my cheek and the encouraging way he told me everything I'd done was right. I didn't have the same ideas about my decisions as he did, but I enjoyed the sentiment all the same. I still worried I'd brought darkness down on everyone I'd come into contact with, even if it was no fault of my own. Father had been right when he'd yelled at me how I should have been grateful for everyone in the compound sacrificing their lives so I'd be safe. I hated thinking that anyone had given everything up to protect me. They should have told me what was at stake. Maybe if they had, then I would have understood and not been such a brat. I would have seen everything for what it was, instead of what I thought it to be. A pretty cage they wanted to keep me in. I sighed as I looked over at Weston. He was doing it too, trying to protect me only without keeping me in a cage. He'd already told me he wouldn't lock me away to save me from the dark. I'd proven I could be useful in a fight. Maybe he would be different. I couldn't really hope for much though. I knew nothing about him.

"Tell me, what role do you play in your pack?" I asked softly as we made our way through the dense snow. He scrubbed a hand over his neck.

"I am more of an outcast among the Snow Wolves." He grinned sheepishly. "I'm a wolf, but I'm also… not. It's hard to explain. That's why they have no control over me." He looked at the ground and kicked a rock.

"What else are you then?" I asked with a furrowed brow. He was the most beautiful wolf I'd ever seen. Surely that meant he ranked at the top of the pack, especially since he was such a fierce fighter. It didn't make sense that he was an outsider the way I had always been. Everyone looked down on me because I wanted to go explore, and I finally realized why. It sucked. I just wanted to be me, not some lost princess destined to save a world I had never known. They'd unknowingly burdened me and caged me so I could rise to be the person they thought I'd be, but in the end the only person I could be was myself.

"I'm something far more dangerous than your average wolf." There was a hint of menace in his smile that caused my breath to hitch. He had been so sweet and nice as we escaped from the compound, and his wolf had been doting on me with gentle licks to make me feel better. Was it all an act? Was he going to take me to the very people who wished to see me harmed? "Don't worry, love. You are safe with me. I will not betray you, but you may not like what happens to anyone who attempts to hurt you. I'm just giving you warning now. I'm much more dangerous than any dark wolf or bear." I shuddered at his words, but warmth filled me at the same time. I trusted him not to hurt me or cage me for protection. I had no idea why, but something just felt right. I grabbed his hand and smiled. His brow furrowed in confusion.

"You may be more dangerous than anything in this realm, but I know you won't hurt me. Now, let's go meet the wolves. I need to know what caused all this craziness since my own family kept me in the dark." I didn't really want to know any more about him until I figured out what the heck was going on in my life and what it meant for my future. Was I really a lost princess from a different realm? What had happened to my mother? Was she killed, or did she turn dark like the beasts who'd attacked us? As sad as it was to think, I hoped it was the former. I remembered the black veins under the bear's skin and didn't wish that taint on my worst enemy. I looked at Weston's leg, hoping it wasn't contagious from a scratch.

"I'm fine, precious. Shifting helped, and I'm much harder to kill than your average shifter." He grinned down at me as he cupped my cheek.

"Why do you call me that?" I whispered.

"Because you hate being called princess, and that is what you are. You are precious, not just to me, but to all the realms. You are the start of bringing balance to the universe." I stared at him with shock in my eyes. That was a lot of pressure to put on one girl who had never been anywhere or done anything in her short life. Could I live up to what everyone thought I would become? The thought scared the living daylights out of me.

"Maybe I'm not who everyone thinks I am. Maybe I'm just a girl and the real princess is out there somewhere. Maybe she is the one who really needs rescuing. Did you think about that?" I was screeching. I was in complete hysterics. I didn't know how to be a princess. The only things I knew how to do were argue about being locked up and defend myself.

"You are the princess, but I will not force you to take the role. That has to be your choice. We will see when we get to the compound, okay? I will never force you to do anything you don't want to do. I may urge you to see a different point of view, but this is your life, and ultimately your decision." He kissed my temple.

"I don't know how everyone is so sure," my voice was small.

"Hold out your hands." He raised an eyebrow when I looked at him in question. "I watched you with the snowflakes, and you made those icicles. Do you think any normal girl could have conjured ice daggers to pierce her enemies?" He grinned, and I could have sworn I saw pride in his smile. It made my insides all gooey.

I smiled back. I hadn't even thought about the icicle missiles that I'd used on those wolves. Had I killed them? Did I care if I had? They were evil. That was the only consolation I had for what I had done. I'd never killed anything before tonight. The only thing I'd ever shot at were targets. I sagged in Weston's arms. What had I done? I balled my fists as I started hyperventilating. Weston turned to me and slid his hands down my arms to my hands before entwining his fingers with mine. He held my hands palm to the sky, and I watched as the snowflakes started to dance. I concentrated on them and they turned into a mini cyclone in my hand.

"Do you think you could do that if you were just a normal girl? You *are* the lost princess. I would bet my life on it, and I promise you I will be there to help you know matter what you decide to do. I will be with you no matter where you decide to go, and I will never let anyone cage you again." He kneeled at my feet with a fist against his heart as he bowed his head. I could feel his vow around my heart, and I gasped.

"What was that?" I shrieked, my eyes wide.

"It was a vow of fealty," a new voice spoke up from the shadows and my hands were up in an instant, icy tendrils swirling around them.

"Who are you?" I snarled.

"My name is Akos, the Alpha of the Snow Wolves and protector of the Ice Queen." He bowed to me and my jaw dropped open.

"Stop. What is happening here?" I breathed heavily, still feeling Weston's vow wrap around my chest. "I know what you said, but how?"

"He swore his life to his Queen," the man said, bowing to me in deference, which caused me to balk.

"What do you mean? I am no one's Queen." I growled in shock.

"Princess Freesia, I'm sorry you have not been raised knowing what you are, but you are the Queen for whom we have been searching for the last seventeen years." The old man bowed low to the ground. What the heck was going on? They were really telling me I was the lost princess. "You need to tell him to rise, or he will stay there all day," the old wolf grinned.

"Weston, please stand. You never have to bow to me. We are equals." I had no idea where the words came from, but when his eyes met mine, I realized how true they were. We were equal in every way, and he would do everything he could to keep me safe. The old wolf, Akos, smiled as I looked at him and bowed again.

"Stand up. I am no princess. You both need to understand that. I'm just Freesia," my voice wobbled and Weston wrapped an around my shoulders, pulling me close.

"You get to decide what you are, but you are still precious to me." He kissed my temple. The Alpha wolf raised an eyebrow at me.

"What?" I shouted at Akos.

"Your guardian never told you who you were?" he asked, aghast.

"No, my guardians told me I was nothing but a burden that they had sacrificed their lives for. They never told me I was the Ice Princess." I glared at the shifter. "Not until tonight, when Athos decided that I was being a spoiled child because I wanted to be free to explore myself and my magic." I could tell this wolf wanted to do the same to me. "West, I want to go away from here." I looked at the man who was still kneeled in front of me. He nodded and led me away from the angry elder. I started to wonder if I had been wrong. My instincts said that no I hadn't been wrong.

"Princess, you must stay within the pack's lands." Akos insisted, but I glared at him as Weston growled.

"You will not cage her Alpha," Weston growled. "She will never be imprisoned again. I will not allow it, not even from you." He glared at the Alpha and I wondered what the Alpha of the Snow Wolves would say to those words.

"I will not cage the Queen. We only wish to protect her as she takes her rightful place on the throne." He ducked his head in deference to Weston. What was Weston to cause this reaction?

"Can you both stop talking about me like I'm not here?" I threw my hands up. Weston pulled me closer, squeezing me tight around the waist.

Sorry, precious, he said inside my head and I turned to look at him. I had thought that was only something he could do in wolf form. *No, love. We will be able to talk like this no matter where we are, or what form I'm in.*

The old wolf was looking at us strangely. "You said you couldn't read my mind." I glared at him.

"You were shouting your thoughts again." I rolled my eyes as he grinned, and the old man scowled.

"You linked with her?" It was an accusation, and one I didn't particularly like. "How could you be so reckless?"

"Watch it," Weston growled. "It's not like I did it on purpose. She's my… " he trailed off and scowled at them both.

"I'm your what? And why do you both continue to talk about me like I'm not standing right here?" I shoved away from Weston, growing more irritated by the second. I clenched and unclenched my fists, trying to keep the anger at bay. A dagger of ice formed in my fist and I dropped it, screaming at the sight. "What the hell was that?" I screeched.

"I told you that you were the Ice Princess." I growled at the smug tone and they both looked at me with shock.

"Ugh, just why? I don't want to be some lost princess that everyone wants to cage," I huffed and dropped to the ground, pouting like a toddler.

"No one is going to cage you, okay?" Weston crouched in front of me and tilted my chin so I would look at him. His steel-gray eyes begged me to trust him, so I nodded, relaxing a bit.

"As touching as this is, we need to get to the compound and alert the pack to what is happening." The old man sneered. I really didn't like him one bit.

"Go on then," Weston snarled. "We'll be right behind you."

6

WESTON

Akos was baiting me. We both knew it. I kept my composure as much as I could, so I didn't scare the princess by showing my true colors. Both parts of me wanted his blood, and they hardly ever agreed on anything. The one thing they were in absolute agreement on was the fact that Freesia was our mate. I couldn't tell her that though, she would only see it as another way to cage her. I'd just met her, and already the fierce need to protect her was almost unbearable.

We walked through the snow, letting the pompous Alpha put distance between us. "What were you going to say back there?" she asked, and I wanted to kick myself for letting the words almost slip out. I couldn't lie to her, but maybe I could give her something else.

"You're not ready to hear it yet. You just got out of the

compound for the first time. Enjoy your freedom for a while, there's time to talk about other things later." I smiled at her confused look and she huffed out a breath in frustration.

"I can handle it," she grumbled, and I couldn't help but chuckle.

"Later, I promise." I looped my hand around her back and pulled her close. I couldn't stop touching her, though I knew I should. Every brush of her skin on mine solidified the bond more, but I just couldn't stop. She nodded her head and smiled that dazzling smile that lit up my insides. My wolf howled in my head, desperate to claim her.

The compound came into view and I saw an irritated Akos waiting for us on the trail, tapping his foot in agitation. Oh well. He could wait all day for all the fucks I had to give.

"Come along, Princess. Your guard will be excited to see that you've come back to us." Akos tried for a kind smile, but it looked more like a grimace. She eyed him warily but continued walking. I could tell what she was thinking, even if I couldn't actually read her mind. I hadn't been lying before, she had been shouting her thoughts at me, but now all was quiet. There was a thin barrier keeping me out. I was impressed. She learned rather quickly. I shouldn't have been surprised or disappointed in the fact that she'd closed off the link. But I rather liked having her scream her thoughts inside my head.

"I haven't come back to anyone. I don't even know what's going on. It seems like I have gone from one cage to another," she spoke softly, but firmly. I glared at the idiotic Alpha. We'd already been over this, and if he challenged my decision to let her leave when she wanted, there would be nothing to stop me from taking his spot as Alpha of the Snow Wolves. I didn't want to, but I would if he interfered in her happiness.

"We will inform you of all you need to know." He waved her forward and as soon as I stepped beside her, he put a hand on my shoulder. "You have brought evil to the wards. I need you to patrol and make sure they hold."

"Not a fucking chance," I growled. We both knew my wolf was stronger. I didn't take orders from the Alpha.

"You endangered us all when you ventured so far out." He glared at me.

"Yeah? And what would have happened to Freesia had I not? Bears attacked her compound. I'm sure they didn't follow me there. The attack was too coordinated. They knew where to find her and had I not been there, we never would have known they'd captured the princess." Freesia's breath caught on a gasp and I wanted nothing more than to tear Akos apart limb by limb for causing me to scare her.

"What about my family?" her voice quivered, and tears shined in her eyes.

"They are all warriors in their own right. They will be fine, and I'm sure Athos will remember what I said about the pack's lands. If there's more trouble, they will come here." I squeezed her to me in a hug, more for her comfort than anything else.

Akos rolled his eyes. "All the more reason for you to watch the perimeter," he scoffed.

"I'll send Jax or Eli. I'm not leaving her alone with you." I glared at the Alpha. There was no way I was letting him separate us. I could see the panic in her eyes when he'd tried to order me away. It wasn't happening.

"Fine. Come on, then. The council is waiting," he grumbled. I grabbed Freesia's hand and squeezed it as we followed behind the disgruntled Alpha. I had a feeling that as long as we were inside the wards, the Alpha would do his best to keep me away from her.

I would have to have the men keep a close watch on the Alpha and Freesia. I wouldn't let him do anything to compromise her, or her safety. I sent a mental message to Jax and Eli. *We need a perimeter sweep. Make sure the wards are secure*, I ordered. I waited to hear their words of confirmation before I tuned out. They would make sure nothing came through the wards while I made sure no one tried to take Freesia away. They would be wise to know that anything they did to pull my mate away from me would fucking destroy them. Starting with the Alpha. I squeezed her hand again, offering comfort even though I could probably use my own.

You okay? I asked telepathically. *We will leave as soon as you want to. You don't have to stay here with the wolves. They will not challenge me.* I meant it to be comforting, but she looked over at me quizzically.

Why won't they challenge you? I thought he was the Alpha. She nodded toward Akos. I nodded.

Yes, but if I wanted to, I could easily become Alpha and the entire pack knows it. If he tries to deceive me, or trap you in any way, I will challenge him for his role as Alpha and he knows it. Her eyes widened in shock before she nodded her head with a small smile.

You don't need to challenge the Alpha for me. I can take care of myself. Her cheeks were tinted pink.

I know you don't need me to. I know you can take care of yourself, but it won't stop me from doing whatever I have to do to make sure you're happy and safe. I had no idea why such declarations kept coming out of my mouth. I wasn't that guy. I was an asshole. Always. Why did I care so much about her happiness? It didn't make any sense.

Well, don't go challenging anyone just yet. She smiled and bumped her shoulder into mine. There was no way I could make that promise, so I inclined my head, and we made our way through the main pack doors. *Here goes nothing*, I thought as we entered the hall. Let the games begin.

FREESIA

We walked into the crowded hall, and despite all the bravado I'd had before, I shrunk closer to Weston. There were so many wolves in there. I hadn't realized the sheer number of people that would be there. *Maybe we shouldn't be here,* I said into Weston's mind. He smiled at me and wrapped his arm around me, instantly comforting me. It was weird I felt so close to someone so quickly, but he'd been nothing but protective of me and my freedom. I didn't want to be separated from him.

The Alpha climbed to a platform where he held out a hand. "Snow Wolves of Avalon I give you the lost princess Freesia of the Court of Ice." A hush fell over the crowd, but their eyes all looked at me inquisitively. It made me angry. Why did he have to make a huge proclamation? Weston stiffened next to me, and I was sure he was just as angry as I was. My fist that wasn't squeezing Weston's hand clenched and unclenched, until once again I had created an ice dagger out of thin air, but this time I didn't drop it. It felt comfortable in my hand, like it could protect me from all the eyes staring at me disappointed that their princess was such a weakling.

Don't let them see you cower. Wolves respect strength, Weston spoke into my mind. I nodded imperceptibly and leaned away from him, holding the dagger like a lifeline as I stood straight and pushed my shoulders back. I could do this. As I looked each of the wolves in the eye, they looked away. All except one man, who leaned against the back wall with a smirk on his face as he nodded at me. There were several other men by him who all nodded to me. Like the guy with the smirk, they were encouraging me to show my strength.

"I told you I won't be caged Alpha, what is the meaning of this?" My voice was strong, and Weston squeezed my hand.

"Protection, cage. It's all in the eye of the beholder. I wish only to keep you protected until you can take our home back from the Dark Fae." He shrugged. Weston growled and the men along the back wall stood at attention.

"No," I said loudly and clearly. "I don't need, nor do I want your protection." I glared at him.

"But," he sputtered. "Our pack has always been the fierce protectors of the Ice Kingdom for centuries."

"And in all those centuries, did you ever try to lock a Queen up to *protect* her?" I raised an eyebrow at him.

"You are ignorant of our world and have only just begun to

use your powers. No Queen in history was ever so vulnerable. We do what we do to protect you and to restore our Kingdom." He sneered at me.

"You sound an awful lot like my mother and Athos who were the ones who locked me up in the first place. I will not be chained just to satisfy your own ends. This power play you're going for right now will fail." I had no idea where the confidence came from, but I noticed the men from the back wall moving in closer. I wasn't sure if they were pack or Weston's people.

They're mine, precious. They are only moving in to keep the guards from rushing in. I felt him whisper across my mind. I nodded.

"We have only come here to rest and recover. You will not keep me here." I glared at the Alpha and he looked completely dumbfounded.

"You don't have the power to stand against me and the entire Snow Wolves pack," he sputtered. The men I'd noticed before stood like a wall in front of me, including Weston, who wrapped his hand behind him and around my back, pulling me close.

"She may not right now, but I do. And it'll only take a short time to hone her powers. Keep talking if you want me to challenge you, Alpha," he growled low in his throat. The man I'd seen smirking from the back wall winked at me over his shoulder, and I rolled my eyes. He just smirked again as he turned his attention back to a sputtering Alpha.

"You wish to keep our Queen from us, her most loyal protectors?" the Alpha scoffed.

"I wish to give her a choice. She has never been given a real choice on what she wants, and my men and I will protect that right, so she never feels chained again." Weston spoke clearly and with authority. "Do not forget yourself, Alpha. We both know I could challenge you and take this entire pack from you. Do. Not. Test. Me. The only reason you are Alpha is because I allow it." He raised an eyebrow and the Alpha's eyes lowered.

"We will respect the princess' wishes until such a time they endanger her safety." His eyes sparkled at the words.

"No, you will respect her choices always, or I will throw down a challenge right now."

"You are a fool. She needs to be hidden away until she is ready to take back her Kingdom."

"I challenge Alpha Akos for leadership of the Snow Wolves pack." I gasped at the words, and Weston looked at the man next to him. The smirking guy. He'd just challenged the Alpha, so Weston didn't have to.

"What are you doing?" Weston whispered harshly.

"Just doing my part, boss." He grinned.

"Luka? You challenge me for the role of Alpha?" Akos looked as confused as everyone else.

"You heard me. I challenge you for the role of Alpha." There was something strange about this person. He adopted a relaxed posture and his ever-present smirk as he continued to challenge the leader of the pack.

"Very well, but I will take no pride in killing you Luka." This was the first time I'd seen Akos look regretful since I'd met him hours before. He didn't relish in the challenge as I'd thought he would.

"Wait, kill?" I screeched, and Luka winked at me over his shoulder again as Weston pulled me in closer to his back. *What is he talking about?* I whispered into his mind.

When someone challenges an Alpha for pack leadership, it's a battle to the death in their wolf forms. There are only two options if a wolf is bested: They submit, which for an Alpha is a fate worse than death, and they are exiled from the pack's lands, or death itself. I gasped at his words. *It's okay, precious. My men are nearly as powerful as I am. Luka will not fail, and he will make the old Alpha submit if possible. He's not out to kill the old man.* I was not comforted by his words. This brutal world I'd found myself in was worse than mother's stories that she'd used to scare me. But I would not allow my fear to show as I watch a big circle form among the crowd. They were seriously going to do it right here? I couldn't get passed the brutality.

Both men stood in the center of the circle and started undressing. I turned my head into Weston's chest embarrassed, and he chuckled. "We aren't embarrassed by nudity around here, but they have both fully changed now," he chuckled against my temple.

"Don't make fun of me." I elbowed him, grinning.

I'm not making fun of you, precious. It's cute you're embarrassed, plus I don't want you looking at anyone naked.

He growled in my head, and I practically melted. What was this feeling I had toward the mysterious Weston? It was as if we were linked on a much deeper level than our minds. It was unlike anything I ever felt before, but I forced myself to stop thinking about it and focus on the Alpha challenge that was happening right in front of me.

The two wolves circled each other, and I gasped at the color of Luka's wolf. It was black as night, much like the wolves who'd attacked us. I clenched my fist, and the ice dagger was there in an instant. "Shhh, you're safe, precious," Weston crooned in my ear. "He was Alpha of the night wolves before they were wiped out by the Dark Fae. He is no threat to you." His hands rubbed up and down my arms. I nodded, even though the words didn't really do anything to make me feel any safer.

"His pack was wiped out by the Dark Fae?" I asked in a small voice, and he nodded against my shoulder. "That must have been horrible."

"It was, but Luka and I have been close for a long time. We only stay with the Snow Wolves to keep up appearances. I can't believe he is challenging the Alpha right now," he sighed.

The two Alphas circled each other continuously, both looking for an opening to take the other down. The white wolf lunged forward, but Luka snapped his jaw against the other wolf's snout, causing red to leak out. *How do we stop this?* I asked Weston inside his head.

There's no way to stop it until one of them submits, or dies.

I'm sorry, precious. I turned my face into his chest, not wanting to watch the brutal display for another second. *If you don't watch, it will diminish the sacrifice, love. They are competing for who gets to ensure your safety.*

What do you mean? I looked up into his face.

Akos thinks the best way to protect you is by keeping you locked up. Luka thinks like me. You can be protected as you're free to roam. They both are fighting to decide who gets the decision on your safety. He shrugged. *If you don't watch. You diminish the ultimate sacrifice.* I turned my head and watched the fight. Akos was getting restless and kept snapping at Luka. Luka slapped at him with huge fangs. Luka snarled and swiped a paw, hitting him in the side and causing the Alpha to yelp as more blood coated his white fur. It didn't seem to deter the Alpha. He just seemed to get more vicious. I wasn't really liking the fact that they were fighting because of me, but I did as Weston said and never took my eyes off the wolves.

Luka stayed on defense, doing everything he could to tire the Alpha out. It seemed to work as he lost more blood and became slower and weaker. Blood coated the floor and the next time Akos lunged, he slid in it, causing him to fall. Luka's jaws clamped on the Alpha's neck and he let out a whimper. At first I thought he was submitting until his paw came up and sliced into Luka's chest. The wolf clamped down harder and shook his head violently until a crack filled the room and Akos' neck snapped, leaving him dangling from Luka's jowls. Dead. I whimpered and Weston pulled me closer. He turned my head so I was pressed into his hard chest.

Murmurs filled the room, but I wasn't listening to their words. I breathed in Weston's scent and it calmed my rattled nerves. He smelled like blizzards and pine. It was comforting. Almost a little too comforting. I had no idea why the man felt like home.

8

WESTON

"Shhh, it's over now," I whispered to Freesia. She trembled in my arms, and a thought flitted through my head about her trembling for different reasons. I needed to shut that down because I knew the first time I had her, I wouldn't be able to stop myself from mating her and she needed to learn more about our world and herself first. I wasn't about to trap her the way everyone else in her life seemed to want to. Luka strutted over to us with a smirk.

"I'm going to be facing one challenge after another with this group. They don't like the idea of a night wolf running their pack." His eyes glittered with amusement. He loved it when people challenged him. "Hello, little princess." He winked at her. I snarled through our link and his smirk grew into a full-blown smile.

"Easy, West. I'm not poaching your girl," the asshole said

out loud, and I wanted to kick his fucking ass. Freesia stiffened and stood a little taller, taking a step away, and I was instantly cold.

"I'm not… we're not," she blushed a pretty shade of pink and looked away. The fucker was enjoying this way too much. I was going to beat his ass fucking bloody for it later. He grinned like he could read my thoughts.

"Bring it," he taunted me in my head. He was high on the adrenaline of fighting Akos. I could tell. He rubbed his hands together gleefully. "Okay, listen up. The princess is given free reign, she can come and go as she pleases as long as Weston, or another of his personal guard are within screaming distance." He looked over at Freesia, who shrugged.

"It's more freedom than I've ever had before. I guess I can't complain." She nodded at him and he continued with a flourish. He was enjoying this way too much.

"Also, you need to learn your magic. There will be a time when we have to fight to get the Kingdoms back, and you will need everything at your disposal to win." A sly smile broke across his features and I was about to step forward to cut off whatever he was about to say, but he beat me to it. "West will teach you. He's the best magic user I know." *Shit*. He was going to die a slow, painful death. The bastard knew what she was to me, and he was putting me in a tough position. Every moment spent with her meant my wolf would push me more and more to claim her. She was my responsibility though, and I couldn't have my men getting too close to her. Luka was truly diabolical.

"I'll teach you," I said to her, smiling past my foul mood and rage at Luka for playing this game.

"Okay, now that's settled. Anything else to go over before we close this meeting?" He glared at each pack member, and they all bared their throats in submission. I grinned. Luka wasn't getting challenged today. He looked a little disappointed, but clapped his hands together and ended the bloody meeting. "Weston, I need to speak with you, privately." He eyed Freesia, and I called out to Ryker in my head. *Please show Freesia to her room. I'll be there after I'm done talking to the pompous asshat who's never going to get over himself now that he's an Alpha again.* Ryker chuckled while Luka flipped me the bird.

"Freesia. This is Ryker. He's going to take you to your room while I have a chat with the new Alpha. There should be things you can change into and a bathroom so you can shower. I'll be there after I find out what the dickhead wants." She giggled at my words and nodded. I followed Luka down the hall in the opposite direction than Ryker was taking Freesia. I didn't like letting her out of my sight so soon after we got there, but I really didn't have much choice and Ryker would protect her with his life. I knew that.

Luka led me into what used to be Akos' office and made himself comfortable behind the huge marble desk and kicked his feet up. Akos would have lost his shit if he were there to see that. "We can all see what's going on with the princess. Are you sure about this?" He raised a brow at me.

I had no idea what he was talking about all I knew was that

I burned for her since the first time I met her. "You're Fae side has already claimed her." I nodded because that was obvious. My wolf was close to doing the same. If he did, then we would be irrevocably bound. There was no use in denying what she was to me.

"I know," I sighed and slumped into the chair in front of him.

"You know, she was betrothed in infancy. If Baskin finds her, he will challenge you for her, which is his right." I knew it was true, and then it hit me.

"Shit, Baskin was one of the guards at the compound. He seemed awfully comfortable just barging into her room." I was irrationally angry thinking about it. She was mine. Not completely, not yet, but she would be. If I had to challenge Baskin, I would. I would do anything for her.

"Do you think there was anything going on between them?" He raised a mocking brow at me.

"No, she would have asked him to come with her if there had been. I'm pretty sure she saw him as just a friend, or another person who sought to cage her, but we will keep an eye out just in case." Luka nodded thoughtfully. I could tell there was more, but he wasn't talking. "Just spit it out already."

"I was just thinking how the Snow Wolves and Athos' clan had always been allies. What happens when he finds out you brought his charge here?" I shrugged because I didn't really give a crap.

"We deal with Athos and his clan when the time comes.

Tell me something. Why did you challenge Akos?" I changed the subject because I didn't want to think about the people who had made her miserable.

"I knew you didn't want to be Alpha, but I could see that you would do it if it meant giving her what she'd always craved, so I took the decision out of your hands." He shrugged. That had been exactly what I had thought he'd been doing.

"Are we done here?" I asked because my skin was itching to get to her. He nodded, and I left without another word.

I made my way through the maze of hallways until I got to the mahogany double doors where Ryker was standing outside. I nodded to him in thanks and he inclined his head. "Sure thing, boss." I grimaced. I hated when he called me that. Knocking on the door, I waited for her to answer. After a few minutes there was still no answer. I looked at Ryker. "She's in there. Maybe she's sleeping? It has been a long night for her." I couldn't take that chance. If Athos found the compound and snatched her away just to treat her like shit again, I would never forgive myself.

Opening the door, I rushed inside and right into a very wet, very naked Freesia. She stumbled and my arms wrapped around her to steady her. The only thing she was wearing was a white fluffy towel. I couldn't help but trace the water with my eyes as it trailed down her chest to the knot of the towel. My arms were still wrapped around her and I heard a cough before Ryker closed the door. "Sorry, I knocked and when you didn't answer, I panicked thinking someone got in here." I smiled sheepishly. Her eyes were wide, and her breath caught. In the light of the room, her blue eyes were almost violet.

"Sorry, I was bathing." She ducked her head away shyly. I wanted nothing more than to rip that towel away and worship her body. I was hard as steel, and it took every ounce of willpower I possessed to step away from her. "I got you all wet," she said, her tone apologetic. I just shrugged.

"It's okay, I'll let you rest. We can start working on your powers in the morning if you'd like?" She nodded but looked a bit reluctant. "I'm in the room right next door, and Ryker is out in the hall if you need him. We aren't going to let anyone come in here and snatch you away. Tomorrow after training we can do a little exploring." Her whole face lit up at the words and I felt a deep sense of pride. I wanted to make her smile like that all the time. Without even thinking about what I was doing, I kissed her cheek and turned to leave.

"Weston?" she called, and I turned back to look at her. "Thank you." I nodded and left the room before I did something stupid.

When I reached my room, I slumped against the door and banged my head back against it, wishing I hadn't gone rushing into her room like an animal. My cock was hard as fuck and I knew if I didn't get some relief, there would be no sleep in my future. It may have been depraved, but I didn't care. I was half Fae, depravity was in my nature.

Making my way to the bathroom, I started the huge stone shower and stripped my dirty clothes. I could have used magic to do it, but I was distracted. The image of her in nothing but a towel, her porcelain skin glistening with water, kept running through my mind. I got in the shower and let the hot water soothe my aching muscles as I fisted my cock. Closing my eyes, I imagined Freesia on her knees in front of me, the hot spray of the shower beating down on her as she opened her mouth to lick my tip. I pushed all the way into her mouth and fisted her hair as I fucked that gorgeous mouth of hers. Tightening my hand, I pumped faster, imagining her moans and the vibrations from them took me over the edge.

9

FREESIA

I had the same dream I'd been having every night since I was ten years old. I was running through a snowy forest laughing as something chased me. I created a snowball out of thin air and threw it over my shoulder at the huge white wolf. The wolf grunted as he picked up speed and lunged for me. The dream evolved from there. The wolf was in midair when he shifted into a man and caught me around the waist. I looked into Weston's steel-gray eyes as he backed me into the tree. "Gotcha." He grinned before bringing his lips down on mine in a heated kiss. I moaned into his mouth, wrapping my arms around his neck, and pulling him closer. "You're mine, precious, and I'm going to mark you in every possible way." He rested his forehead against mine and kissed my nose lightly.

The dream faded, and I groaned. I wasn't ready to get up

yet. I hadn't wanted that dream to end. What could it all mean, though? I'd always felt such freedom and happiness in that dream, but now there was more. *Weston.* I sighed and sat up. There was a knock on the door, and I rushed to open it. Disappointed when it was a woman pushing a cart with what must have been breakfast. I smiled and thanked her. There was so much food on the cart, I didn't know where to start. My eyes bulged, and I heard a soft chuckle from the open doorway.

"Mind if I join you?" Weston asked, and my mouth watered for a totally different reason. His black shirt was pulled tight over his rippling muscles. His dark hair had that just out of bed look. His stormy eyes glinted in the light and for a second I forgot to breathe.

"Yeah, um, sure. There is more food than I can eat here." I smiled awkwardly. He grinned at me and I nearly tripped over my own feet. What the heck was wrong with me? I never reacted like this. Weston reached out to steady me. His big hands landed on my hips, and I flushed.

"You okay?" he whispered next to my ear, and my whole body broke out into goosebumps. Was it just the dream causing me to react this way to him? No, I didn't think so. He was by far the most gorgeous man I'd ever seen.

"I-I'm fine." I tried to smile, but I couldn't make my body move with him so close. He had his chest pressed into my back and I heard an almost imperceptible groan from him as he took a step back. I was instantly cold.

"Right, so breakfast and then we will work on your magic." He stepped around me, grabbing a plate and holding it out to me. Taking the plate, I grabbed a few of my favorite breakfast foods. The bacon and sausage smelled heavenly. I grabbed a glass of juice and headed to the small table on the other side of the room. Weston followed my lead, but he had his plate piled much higher than my own. "How did you sleep?" he asked as he sat down next to me at the tiny table.

"I slept great. That bed is really comfortable." I blushed bright red when I realized what I had said. My mind went to the bed and Weston, and I was suddenly too hot. He chuckled and my eyes snapped to his.

"Where did your mind go there, precious?" He grinned, and it was full of mischief. I wondered if he was feeling the same things. He'd been so sweet and attentive the day before. I hadn't really been looking at him like a man, but now? It was hard not to.

"Nowhere?" I looked away, wanting to kick myself for framing it as a question.

"That pretty blush says different." His eyes darkened as he placed one finger under my chin and turned me so I had to look at him. His thumb came up and caressed my cheek where I was sure my skin resembled a tomato.

"It was nothing." I looked away from him. "I had a strange dream and I think it's still affecting me." I shrugged.

"Oh? I had a pretty great dream. I was running through the forest chasing a beautiful princess who kept throwing snow-balls at me." I gasped at his words and turned to look at him. He hadn't been in my head, had he? He'd told me he couldn't read my mind.

"What did you say?" I whispered in complete shock and he looked at me confused.

"I was telling you about my dream." He scrunched his brows in confusion.

"Are you sure you can't read my mind? That isn't funny." I started to get upset and frost coated my fingers.

"What are you talking about, precious?" He grabbed my hands, not even wincing from the cold.

"I have had that same dream every night for the last eight years. Tell me how you knew about it," I demanded.

"Eight years? You had *that* dream at ten years old?" His face was a mask of shock.

"Well, it has evolved since then. When I was younger, it was just the snowballs and the chasing. Now it's something much more, uh, let's say heated?" I groaned at my own words.

"You dreamed of me every night for eight years?" He was missing the point.

"Yes," I said shyly. "Well, your wolf anyway."

"I dreamed of you, too." His whisper was so low I almost thought I'd imagined it.

"What?" I asked, looking over at him with wide eyes.

"I'm not sure how long it's been because I have lived for several centuries, but I have been dreaming of you for a long time, though before last night I could never see your face, only hear your tinkling laugh as you pelted me with snowballs," he chuckled. I was so confused. What was going on here?

"What does this all mean?" I asked hesitantly.

"I don't know, precious. You care to see where it goes

though?" He looked at me from beneath his lashes and my insides somersaulted. Yes, I definitely wanted to see where this would go. I didn't care that I was being reckless. I wanted Weston, and I wasn't going to apologize for it. I nodded. His smile was brilliant as he kissed my cheek.

"Eat your breakfast. You're going to need the energy for what I have planned." He winked at me and I giggled before going back to my food, wondering what he had planned. Would he teach me to create snowballs out of thin air so we could recreate the dream? I grinned as I finished eating and he grabbed my hand, pulling me out of my chair and leading me to the door. "You ready for your first magic lesson?" he asked, and I nodded. I was excited for someone to show me how to use magic.

We went outside to what looked like an outdoor training center with weapons lining the high stone walls. It looked like an arena. He led me to a small clearing off to the right where we could use defensive magic. Ryker was waiting for us, smirking like he had a secret. I blushed again. It seemed like I did that a lot around this group of men.

"Tell me what you were feeling when you created the ice dagger," Weston whispered close to my ear. He was entirely too close if he wanted me to think about anything other than his firm chest against my back. My fingers tingled as I felt the vibration of his chuckle on my neck.

"I was angry." The words were a breathy whisper.

"Try to recreate that anger and everything you did when

you created the dagger." He was still entirely too close for me to concentrate.

"I can't when you're standing so close." I took a step away from him and he chuckled again. The man knew what he was doing to me and he enjoyed it. I either wanted to beat him with a snowball or wrap myself around him and kiss him. Shoot. Where had that come from? My hand tingled, and I told the buzzing to create a snowball. A perfect snowball sat in my palm seconds later, and I whirled around so fast Weston didn't even see it coming before it smashed in his too perfect face. Ryker roared with laughter behind me as Weston sputtered.

"Oh, precious, you're going to pay for that," he said, stalking toward me. I backed away, but suddenly there was a wall at my back. I tried to make another snowball, but nothing happened. I sidestepped Ryker who wasn't playing fair and started to run, but only made it a few steps before Weston lunged for me and we both went tumbling to the ground. In midair he spun us so I would land on top of him. He smiled up at me as he tucked a stray hair behind my ear. "Now, why would you go and throw a snowball at me like that?" I tried to move away, but his arms were like a vice around my waist.

"You were toying with me. I don't like it," I huffed. In an instant he spun us around and he was on top of me, looking down at me with something swirling in those steel-gray depths of his.

"I would never toy with you, precious. Your magic is tied to your emotions. We need to figure out a way for you to use it in an instant." He looked down at my lips and I subconsciously licked them, causing a low growl to escape him. I wondered if he'd kiss me when I heard a subtle cough somewhere nearby and remembered we weren't alone and were supposed to be training. "No more throwing snowballs at me." He kissed my cheek and helped me up off the ground.

"I make no promises," I smirked.

"Just remember, every time you do, it will end the same way." He winked at me. That was exactly what I was hoping for.

10

The pretty little princess was trying to kill me. If it hadn't been for Ryker's subtle reminder that we were out in the open on the training field, I might have done something bad. Knowing that she'd had the same dream that I'd been having for years, made me insane. I'd almost kissed her as her warm, tight body lay beneath me in the snow, and I knew one kiss from her would never be enough. Shit. I was a goner.

"Okay, think about the anger you felt when you created the dagger. You did it twice when Akos decided you needed to be kept in the compound." I could see the concentration on her face, but her skin was still flushed. "Do you feel the magic buzzing below your skin? It's there, just waiting for you to tell it what to do. Don't force it. Just let it flow and tell it what to do."

I put my hands on her shoulders, and she relaxed visibly. I could feel the vast power pulsing beneath her skin, just waiting for her to direct it. "Now, do what you did when you created the dagger. What was your posture like? What were you doing with your hands?" I watched as she clenched and unclenched her fists several times. Her eyes closed as she concentrated. "Open your eyes for me, precious. You won't be able to close them and concentrate in the midst of a battle." I couldn't stop myself from breathing her in. She smelled of storm clouds fresh snow and something uniquely her. It was intoxicating.

"I did it," she squealed excitedly. I hadn't even realized I'd closed my eyes to breathe her in.

My smile was automatic as I looked down at the two daggers in her hands. They were the perfect size and weight for her small hands. "Great job, beautiful. Do you want to test them out?" She nodded excitedly, bouncing on the balls of her feet. She was so damn cute. I wanted to kiss her so fucking badly.

We're training, boss. Ryker reminded me through our link, and I sent him a mental middle finger. He shook his head, chuckling to himself.

"I know that. Don't go easy on her, she has been training with weapons her whole life, but if you hurt her, I will dismember you," I hadn't realized I'd said the words out loud until her eyes widened in shock. "Don't worry, precious, they will grow back. It's just a long agonizing process."

"Okay, let's not dismember people just because I got a

scratch, Weston." She raised a brow and Ryker laughed before pulling out his obsidian daggers.

"Fine." I nodded reluctantly, but Ryker knew that was not an idle threat. If he put any wounds on her body, I would be out for blood.

"I'm not going to hurt the princess. This is why you chose me for this. I have much better control than the other men." I inclined my head because he was right, but my protective instinct toward her had my hackles up. They circled each other a few times before Ryker struck first. Freesia lifted her blade, and the ice shattered on impact, sizzling under the obsidian blade. Freesia yelped and took a step back, cradling her palm.

Rushing over, I pulled her palm into mine and saw the burn. Ryker's daggers were deadly, but they shouldn't have melted the ice and burned her the way they had. "Are you okay? I'll kill him," I growled.

"No, I'm fine. Look, it's already healing." She was staring at her palm in wonder. "Is my magic doing that?" She looked at me curiously.

"Probably, do you feel it buzzing around the burn?" I asked, still watching as it faded away.

"Yes, it's like a cool balm on the burnt skin." She was still staring at her hand.

"Ice daggers are obviously not good for hand to hand combat. Only for throwing unless you can make them stronger," Ryker mused. "Since you can make them at will, throwing them wouldn't be a problem. You just have to make sure you keep your energy levels up. It can be tiring to use so much magic. Make another one and throw it at me."

"What? I'm not throwing a dagger at you," she said aghast.

"Princess, I won't get hurt. I'm much harder to kill than most." He winked.

She mumbled something under her breath about stupid cocky males, but did as he asked. The blade exploded against his dual daggers. "Again. You need to be faster," he barked.

They did it again and again until the sun was high in the sky and Freesia had sweat dripping down her face. It reminded me of the night before when she had been glistening with water on her cheeks, flushed and wrapped in nothing but a towel. A throat cleared and I looked up at Ryker, whose eyes danced with glee. "That's enough for today. You're great with the daggers, princess, you just need to work on your speed with the magic. We'll teach you, though." The bastard winked as he strutted away.

"You ready for lunch? I thought we could eat in the garden?" I wrapped my arms around her, squeezing lightly.

"Did you see that?" she squealed and threw her arms around my neck. "I must have made a hundred ice daggers, and I didn't even get tired. This is amazing." She had a genuine smile of excitement on her face as she bounced. The only thing I could focus on was her lips so close to mine. My fingers came up to tangle in the white blonde strands of her hair, and I tugged until her head tilted toward me. Her breath hitched as she looked into my eyes. I was a bad, bad man because I wasn't going to stop myself from tasting her lips this time. This was very bad, but I didn't really give a fuck as I brushed my lips across hers, tentatively. Once our lips touched, a zing traveled through me from the place where our flesh met. I couldn't hold back from pressing harder and licking at her lips. She tasted of the sweetest berries and when she moaned, her lips parted for me.

I deepened the kiss and my mind went blank. It was much better than the dream. Her taste burst across my tongue and I growled. I could tell she had never been kissed before, so I tried my best to slow it down, but my whole body was on fire from her touch. When I pulled away, she was flushed and looked disappointed. I was kicking myself for letting things get out of hand, but with Freesia smiling so shyly at me, I couldn't beat myself up too much. I was on top of the world.

"Lunch?" I cleared my throat. I still had my arms around her, and I slid my fingers up her arms to link with hers around my neck, and pulled her hands down to my lips. I kissed each palm before releasing one hand and leading her to the garden.

It wasn't much of a garden. More like a Courtyard with ice sculptures every few feet. There was a table set up in the center next to a fountain. I had no idea why there was a frozen fountain in the middle of the Courtyard that didn't work, but wolves were strange.

"It's beautiful," Freesia breathed as she looked around at all the sculptures. It was ironic to me they had sculptures of ice in the shape of flowers and things you would find in warmer temperatures. I wasn't looking at the intricate designs, though. I couldn't take my eyes off Freesia.

"C'mon let's sit." I pulled her to the cozy little table and pulled her chair out for her. Her cheeks pinked as she sat, and I moved to my seat. The food smelled great, and we both dug in. She looked surprised by her own hunger. "You used a lot of magic today. It's your body telling you to build more energy stores." I nodded to her half-eaten plate.

"Oh, so being starved after using magic is normal?" I nodded to her question, and she grinned. "Glad to know I don't look like a giant hog eating everything in sight."

"You could never look anything but beautiful. Even when you're stuffing your face." I ducked as she threw a carrot at me. We both laughed. "Hey, that was a compliment."

"That was for the stuffing my face part." She mock glared at me, and I couldn't help but chuckle. The amazing lunch with the girl I was clearly falling for was cut short with a damned annoying Luka using our link.

We have company. He sounded pissed, and I cursed.

Who? I asked through the link.

Athos and Baskin. They want the princess. And they are causing quite a scene. I could hear him chuckling.

They can't have her, so they can fuck off. They want to keep her a prisoner. I will kill them all before I let them treat her like that again. I growled out loud.

"What's wrong?" Freesia looked up from her lunch with concern.

"They're here." I shook my head at her look of horror. I didn't ever want to put that look on her face.

"I thought you said it was safe. That the wards would keep them out?" She looked around like something would jump out at us any second, and her fingers started to get those telltale ice crystals on them.

"No, precious. Not the baddies. Athos and Baskin are here kicking up a fuss. They had always been allies to the Snow Wolves, so the wards recognize them as such." I sighed.

"No. That's worse. I have freedom for the first time. Don't let them take me away." She reached out and squeezed my hand. I winced because I had no intention of letting them go anywhere with her, but I couldn't stop them without alienating our own allies.

"Hey? I already told you that I'm not going to let anyone cage you again. You don't have to do anything you don't want to, okay?" I pulled her up into my arms. I would challenge them both at the same time before I let them force her into anything she didn't want.

"I guess exploring is out." She grimaced.

"I'm sorry. I honestly thought we would have some time before they found us, but don't worry. I'll take care of it." I kissed her forehead, and we walked hand in hand to the pack meeting room. Luka and Ryker were smirking where they stood behind my men. This could not be good.

"Freesia. What is the meaning of this?" Athos looked like he was about to explode when he looked down at our joined hands. "What are you doing with my daughter, mutt?"

"You really wanna go there, Athos?" I raised an eyebrow. "No one forced her to be here, and from what I can see, she is not your daughter."

"I raised her." He sputtered.

"Did you, though? Did you ever let me go outside? Did you stop *mother* from torturing me and Molly with stories to keep us contained?" Freesia's hand went cold in mine as she got angrier by the minute.

Easy, precious. Your magic is responding to your distress. I used our link to soothe her. I wasn't sure I was doing such a great job as it got so cold, even I almost had to pull away.

"I'm not distressed. I am pissed." I looked over at her, shocked. I had never heard her use words like that before. She seemed so innocent, but maybe my girl had some claws on her.

"Freesia, come with us. You don't belong here." Baskin stepped forward, and the pleading look he was giving her told me he knew exactly what he'd been promised. A growl left my throat in warning. "Calm down, mutt."

"I'm way more than a wolf and you damn well know it, Baskin, so maybe you should back the fuck off." I glowered at him. Ready to rip him apart if he got too close. "Do not test me, boy," I growled.

"Everyone stop." She glared at the entire group of Alpha males. "I'm perfectly happy where I am, and no one is ever going to dictate what I do again." She narrowed her eyes at Athos and Baskin.

"Freesia." Athos was still an ugly shade of eggplant and

looked like he was about to grab her and take off. He blew out a breath before changing his tactics. "Your mother and sister are worried about you."

"Is mother actually worried? She's not my mother and has never made me feel like I was hers. She seemed to relish in trying to scare me into staying inside the compound. My only regret is Molly. She deserves better." Freesia sneered.

"Where is Akos?" Athos roared.

"Dead." Luka shrugged, looking at him with deadly intent.

"Figures you mutts would take over as soon as you found her. What do the wolves think of you taking over the clan?" Baskin grumbled. Luka stood immediately at his words and walked forward.

"They are more than welcome to challenge me if they think they won't suffer the same fate as their former Alpha, but *I* defeated *him* and proclaimed the princess would be free as long as she had certain protections in place. They *all* submitted to my power, so try again little boy." Luka smirked. "Unless you think to challenge me."

Too far Luka, I said through our link, but all the bastard did was wink.

He's a babe. Not even Athos would allow him to challenge me. He shrugged, and I shook my head. This was getting out of hand.

"Enough," I roared. Everyone turned to look at me. I could feel the power buzzing beneath my skin, waiting to be released. "This is Freesia's decision. If she wants to go with you, we won't stop her, but if you try to take her by force, I *will* destroy you."

Her eyes widened briefly before I saw the resolve cross them. If she decided to go back with them, I would support her decision, for now, but if she decided to stay, there would be a fight.

"Princess. You don't know what he is. You are much safer at the compound where we can look after you." Baskin never should have opened his stupid mouth. He sealed his own fate with those words.

"Really? So you can what? Contain me? I'm tired of being a prisoner. I don't care who you think you are, I'm staying here. They let me go outside," she gasped like it was unheard of. "And in less than a day I've already started to learn about my magic, which is more than any of you did for me." She glared at the fucking idiot, who realized instantly that he'd said the wrong thing. I noticed the second what he thought of as his winning ace occurred to him, and I took a step closer to Freesia.

"We are betrothed," he roared. "What you want doesn't matter. You are mine, and I'm taking you home to the compound." Quicker than I could stop her, Freesias hands shot out and Baskin froze. He was like a living ice sculpture. Freesia cried out in panic and I wrapped my arms around her, murmuring soft words to calm her.

"What have I done?" She sniffled.

"Shhhh, it's okay. He will thaw out and be perfectly fine, if not a little cold." I pulled her close, but she looked up at me with confusion.

"He'll be okay?" she asked in a small voice, and I nodded. I would make sure of it before I sent him back to his compound alone.

"Yes, precious. He will be fine. But Athos looks like he's about to pop a blood vessel in his forehead." She giggled at my words.

"He speaks the truth, Freesia. You were betrothed to him as an infant. You will one day have to marry him." Athos didn't even have the decency to look apologetic.

"Am I the Ice Princess?" she asked in a hard voice and he nodded. "Then I will be Queen, right?" He nodded again. "Then I don't have to answer to you, or him, or anyone else, and I will not marry a tyrant. You can both go back to the compound and stay away from me." She turned and ran from the room. I cursed as I started after her.

"She's not yours, hybrid. She will eventually realize where she belongs, and when she does, she will hate you." Athos was gloating, even though he'd lost. I sent a mental note to Ryker to go after Freesia as I squared off with Athos.

"You know, maybe if you and your people hadn't made her feel like a burden you were forced to bear, she wouldn't despise your home so much, and never would have left. Now, unless you wish to challenge me, I'm going to go after my mate." The words came out unbidden and Athos eyes widened. I thought he was going to argue, but he just stood there as I stomped away.

Where is she? I sent Ryker through the link.

She's in her room. I can hear her crying, boss. He sighed through the link. I could tell he was already starting to care about her, and I didn't know how I felt about that.

I'm on my way, I growled.

When I got to her room I knocked, and I heard a soft "go away" before I pushed through the unlocked door. I took off my shoes and crawled behind her on the bed and pulled her into my arms.

"Shhhh, precious, it's okay. No one is letting them take you if you don't want to go." I pulled her close, so my chest was pressed against her back. My own insecurities surfaced just for a second. "Do you want to go? Do you want to be with Baskin?" I knew I'd said the wrong thing as soon as the words left my mouth.

"What?" She turned in my arms and looked at me with angry eyes. "Are you trying to get rid of me already?" She looked hurt.

"The fuck? Hell no. I'm giving you options. I don't ever want to trap you. I'm just telling you that no matter how much it would hurt me, I would let you go if that was what you wanted." I kissed her nose. She giggled. "Are you better?" I pulled her body to me so her chest was flush with mine and I could feel her heartbeat fluttering against mine.

"Thank you. I just thought maybe I was more trouble than I was worth for the pack." She ducked her head, and I lifted her chin with my fingers.

"I'm not entirely pack, and neither are my men. Make no

mistake we run this place and I promise you, as long as you're with us, we will protect you from physical as well as mental threats. If you want Athos and Baskin gone, they will be gone by morning." I vowed.

"No one has ever cared so much for my happiness." She ducked her head again.

"I'm sorry for what they did." I was getting angrier the longer we continued talking. I wanted to rage at the people who pretended they cared about her.

"It's not your fault. You have been nothing but wonderful. I'm sorry lunch got cut short. It was the first time I had ever gotten to eat outside, among other things." She blushed and buried her face into my chest. Gods, she felt good in my arms.

"I wish I'd found you sooner," I whispered to her as I pulled her impossibly closer.

"Would we be where we are now if you had?" she asked softly, and I had no answer for her. She looked at me expectantly as I sagged shaking my head sadly as I realized nothing would have been the same..

11

FREESIA

I watched him as he weighed his next words. We both knew had he found me as a child, we would most likely not have been in the same position we were in that moment. "No." He shrugged off my question.

"So all the regrets don't matter." I boldly kissed his stubbled chin, and it tickled my lips, causing me to giggle.

"Your happiness means everything," he breathed, kissing my forehead. I felt more cherished in that moment than I'd ever felt, and I knew my answer to his earlier question.

"I don't want to go back with them. I want to stay here with you. I don't understand this connection we have, but I know it feels right. Nothing in that compound ever felt real or right." I grinned when his eyes turned heated.

"I could tell you what this connection is, but I'm afraid it would scare you." He shook his head sadly.

"You don't scare me, Weston." I moved against him, thinking that would make him see how serious I was, but it just caused him to groan and move away. I felt bereft without his comforting warmth. "What's wrong?"

"Nothing, I just don't want to explain this and I'm afraid I'm gonna mess it all up." He shook his head, sitting up on the bed. He propped his elbows onto his bent knees and held his head in his hands.

"Can you please just tell me?" I laid a hand on his back, and his breath caught in his throat.

"My kind, we mate for life. Once we find our true mate, no one else will ever be enough. I knew from the first moment I saw you playing with snowflakes you were mine, but I was scared to tell you because I didn't want you to think I was trying to trap you. Even after discovering we've been sharing dreams since you were a child, I could not do it. It would liter-ally kill me if you walked away. But if that was truly what you wanted, then I would do it just to be sure you were happy." He looked over at me and I wasn't sure what the look in his eyes meant. It looked like equal parts anguish and hope. I didn't know what to say to him. It was a lot to process. I wrapped my arms around him awkwardly and he moved me so I was sitting on his lap.

Wrapping my arms around him, I buried my face in his neck and just breathed him in. This day had started so wonder-fully but had become exceedingly stressful. I needed comfort, and Weston seemed to know that. We sat there for a long time as he rubbed soothing circles on my back. "I'm not trying to make you a prisoner, but I don't want you to be alone while they are here. I don't trust Athos not to take you against your will." He kissed my shoulder. I nodded into his neck because that was exactly what they would try. I didn't want to be alone. "We should probably go back and tell Athos your decision," he sighed, but didn't move to get up.

"We probably should," I groaned, not wanting to move either. "Do you think I'll have to freeze him, too? That was so scary. I didn't know I could do that." I shook my head.

"We will figure out everything you can do, I promise. You will be a formidable Ice Queen when the time comes." He grinned at me. "Now let's go before he gets passed my men and starts searching the compound for you. I don't want him to know where you sleep." He picked me up and set me on my feet before jumping off the bed and grabbing my hand. He kissed my knuckles lightly before leading me from the room.

Ryker walked ahead of us and I found myself wondering what these men were. I knew they weren't entirely pack, but something dark and mysterious lurked beneath the surface. The other wolves were scared of them. I watched them cower if they got too close. I had no reason to fear them, though. They had shown me nothing but kindness.

We walked back into the pack meeting room and my eyes widened when I saw a furious Baskin sitting in a chair wrapped in a blanket, shivering. I smirked. He deserved what he got for trying to tell me what to do. His eyes blazed with anger, but I could finally see the humor in what I had accidentally done. He was fine. "How did they thaw him out so fast?" I giggled. The glare he sent my way made it known that he'd heard me, but I just shrugged.

"You try to take her out of here by force again, Baskin, and what she did will look like child's play," Weston warned, squeezing my hand. Baskin tracked the movement, and the scowl deepened.

"So, that's it, then. You're just gonna throw away a life-long friend for some hybrid?" He spat the words, and I felt Weston's body tense next to mine. Ryker was still standing in front of me, but slightly to the side so I could see the room. Luka was sitting in the Alpha chair, his ever-present smirk on his face as he watched the scene with amusement. He caught me watching him and winked at me. I shook my head, trying to hide a smile.

"You like these, things? They are all a bunch of filthy hybrids." I hadn't noticed how close he'd gotten while I was looking around the room. Ryker took a small step in front of me, putting a hand on Baskin's chest to push him back. He snarled as he reached for me. Weston's hand shot out and grabbed his wrist.

"You are stupid to try that shit again. Do you want to be a permanent ice sculpture? We could place you in the garden with the rest of them. You do not touch her unless she wants you to. By the way that she is standing here letting us stop you, I would say you should back the fuck off." He flung

Baskin's wrist away as Ryker shoved him back and he stumbled lightly.

"I want you both to leave, now. We were going to give you until morning so Baskin could thaw, but since that is done, there is no reason for you to stay." I rolled my shoulders back and held my head high. They couldn't force me to do anything I didn't want to. I had complete confidence in that.

"You would just kick us out?" Athos looked to Luka.

"She will be Queen. She outranks even me. We have always been the loyal protectors of the Ice Monarchy. If she wishes for you to go, so be it." He shrugged, clearly enjoying the entire charade in front of him.

"She is still just a child. She's not ready to be Queen over her people," Athos growled, and I'd had enough.

"And who's fault is that? Huh? You kept me in the dark, imprisoned me, and then expect me to be grateful to you because of the burden I was to you and your family? You expect me to want Baskin, who was complicit in my imprisonment? Hell no." I heard Weston chuckle as Athos' eyes grew wide. I never swore. Mother said it wasn't ladylike, and I didn't want her punishments if I didn't do exactly as she said. I needed to stop thinking of her that way. That woman wasn't my mother. She'd only ever been my torturer.

"The mongrels are already corrupting her," Baskin yelled, throwing his hands up in the air. "You need to leave with us, now princess."

"No, you are leaving. I'm staying. Get over yourself, Baskin.

I will never marry you. I don't even want to be in the same room as you, and unless you both want to be frozen again and placed in the garden, I suggest you leave." I glared at them both.

"This isn't over, princess. You will be mine," he said as he stomped from the room.

"You're making a mistake, Freesia. Don't make enemies out of allies." Athos shook his head as he was escorted from the room. I sagged as they left the room. I hadn't wanted to be so harsh with them, but why couldn't they understand this was my life, and I wasn't going to let them run it anymore?

Weston rubbed his hand up and down my back in a comforting gesture. I looked up at him with a weak smile. "Did I just ruin everything? When the time comes to take back the Kingdom, am I going to have more enemies than allies?"

"They will calm eventually and do what's right for the good of the Kingdom. Athos was your mother's most trusted advisor. He will not endanger the Kingdom because you didn't do what he wanted." Weston was so close to my ear, I could feel his hot breath on my neck. It caused me to shiver.

"I'm sorry, princess, but you will need round-the-clock protection." I opened my mouth, but Luka raised a hand indicating I should let him finish before I decided whether I wanted to blast him or not. "I can't keep them out of pack lands. The wards recognize them as allies, but that doesn't mean you can't still explore and learn to use your magic. The men will stay at a safe distance. It's a precaution I must insist on to make sure your wishes to remain here are respected."

I nodded because I wouldn't put it passed them to try to

take me away. Baskin had tried to grab for me twice. I couldn't get the sight of his enraged face out of my mind. Yes, I definitely needed protection from him. I didn't want to be anywhere near him. If we couldn't keep him out, guards were the next best thing. "Okay, I get it."

12

WESTON

I could tell she hated the idea, but she was smart enough to understand these men were very much a threat to her happiness. They may not hurt her physically, but they had already deeply hurt her mentally. I wouldn't allow that again. I doubled the patrol on the wards and called Jax and Eli back to help Ryker guard my mate. I needed to stop thinking of her like that. She hadn't said anything when I'd told her the truth about the bond we had. She wasn't mine yet, and I refused to push her into something she wasn't ready for.

We walked to her room and I was glad that the cart of food was already there. Lunch had been cut short, and it had been hours since they'd shown up to ruin our fun. The lights were low, giving off a romantic vibe. I sent a mental fuck you to Eli who set up dinner. All I got was a chuckle in response. They were like a bunch of meddling old ladies.

Freesia's eyes widened as she took in the room. Her breath caught when she saw the moon flowers set on the table in a vase. She'd probably never seen real flowers before, and I was pretty sure Eli had conjured them from thin air. It was why they were in full bloom, even though the moon wasn't out yet. I was going to punch him in the throat the next time I saw him. Meddling bastard.

"It's beautiful," she breathed, looking over at me with watery eyes. She reached up on her tiptoes and kissed me softly. I couldn't help the groan that left me as I put my hands on her hips and pulled her closer. She was everything good in this world. I wanted nothing more than to make her mine.

Breaking the kiss, I smiled at her and led her to the table. I pulled out her chair for her to sit while I got the domed covered plates from the cart and set them on the table. Freesia was looking closely at the flowers in the center. The white blossoms were perfect, and she reached her hand out to brush gentle fingers on the petals. "They're so soft."

"They're moon flowers. They only bloom when the moon is high in the sky." I shrugged. Her brows creased together as she looked out the balcony windows.

"How then?" She chewed her lips. Gods, she was adorable.

"I suspect someone used magic so they could meddle." I grinned at her blush. "But if it's flowers you want, I will have some delivered to your room daily." Her eyes widened and her blush deepened. "Let's eat and then you can rest."

"Right," she sighed, and I hated hearing the resignation in her voice.

"It's okay, I'm not going anywhere. I planned to shift and sleep on the floor in front of the balcony doors." She nodded, but didn't say anything else as she started eating. I wanted to ask her what was wrong and beg her to tell me all her secrets, her desires, and everything else. I wanted her in every way, but I had to continue to hold myself back. She needed time, and that was what I planned to give her. Even if it killed me.

We finished eating in silence. I hated that she was feeling sad. "I'm going to the bathroom to shift, okay? If anything happens, yell for me, precious. Ryker is on the other side of the door and Jax is at the bottom of the balcony to make sure no one can get in." I kissed her forehead and walked to the bathroom, closing the door behind me and slumping against it with a huff.

Quickly, I undressed and folded my things to set on the vanity. It took a mere second to shift into my wolf form. Padding on light feet, I smacked the handle with my paw, causing it to turn and the door to open. Freesia was standing there in the tiniest shorts I'd ever seen. Her long-toned legs had my mouth watering as I slowly perused her body with my eyes. The tank top she wore was thin, and I could just make out the outline of her breasts in the dim light. My wolf growled. He wanted to take his mate right then and there. I was feeling the same, only I worked off more than instinct.

Precious, please get in bed. I don't know how long I can hold myself back with you looking like that. I moaned into her mind. I was begging her not to make this situation harder than what it was. It was excruciating to be around my mate all the time and not be able to act on my instincts.

She smiled shyly and walked to the bed before getting under the covers and patting the bed beside her. "You don't have to sleep on the floor, Weston."

You don't understand, precious. I really, really do. Not just to protect you from Baskin, but to protect you from me. She pouted at my words but didn't push as she laid on her side facing the balcony doors. I padded to the doors and curled up in front of them and just watched her for a few minutes before my eyelids grew heavy and sleep claimed me.

The dream was the same as it had been every night for more years than I could count. I was chasing after my perfect blonde princess as I purposely let her pelt me with snowballs. She was so happy and her tinkling laugh sounded like music to my ears every time she hit me. The only difference in the dream now was I could see her face, her gorgeous blue-violet eyes danced with happiness as I was coming to my favorite part. The snowball hit me in the face and my wolf yipped with glee as I lunged for Freesia, shifting midair to wrap my arms around her soft body. She laughed as I pulled her close and her breath hitched when I turned her and backed her into the nearest tree.

My hands were on her hips as I leaned down and claimed her mouth with my own. She moaned and wrapped her arms around my neck, pulling me impossibly closer. She gasped as she remembered that every part of me was bare.

"You're naked," she moaned as I nipped her neck, placing lingering kisses and licks up the column of her throat.

"Yes," I groaned as her hands explored my chest. "Just say the word, precious, and you will be naked too. I will mark every part of you as my own."

"Mmm," she whimpered as my hands moved up under the flimsy top she was wearing to touch the creamy skin of her abdomen. I slid my hands around to her back and down to her ass. Her legs wrapped around my hips as I lifted her, and I pushed her into the tree as I continued to suck and nip at every bit of her exposed skin. My cock was pulsing and hard as steel as she rubbed her jean clad pussy over me.

"Tell me now if you don't want this, beautiful, because if we do this, it's for forever. You will be mine, and I will be yours for eternity." I groaned as she continued to rock her hips.

"I want you. I want this. Please," she cried out in surprise when her clothes vanished. "Neat trick," she moaned.

"It's a dream, precious. I can do anything I want to you." I brought my mouth down on her perfect nipple, sucking it into my mouth. Jesus, even in a dream she tasted like heaven.

"Oh, yeah," she sounded unsure, and I stopped, looking up at her with a slight frown.

"What's wrong?" I asked. We were clearly dream walking, which wasn't unheard of for mates of my kind, but I wondered if she thought there would be real-world implications. "Nothing we do in this dream will be permanent, love. You will still be able to take your time to decide what you want. I won't force you; I swear it." I felt the band tighten around my heart. I'd made a vow to her not to push her. I didn't want to tell her that vow would carry over. It was true our mating in the dream wouldn't affect anything, but a vow as strong as the one I'd just made was unbreakable. I would rather die than break that promise.

"Fuck me, Weston," she groaned as her mouth came down on mine.

"Where did that dirty mouth come from?" I chuckled, but I'd be lying if I said it wasn't hot as fuck to hear her swear like that.

My cock throbbed as I carried her over to a meadow with soft grass and laid her out on the ground. I got my first glimpse of her naked body and nearly came from how sexy she looked as she watched me with those innocent eyes. I tweaked her nipple and her back arched as a loud whoosh of air left her. My hands traveled down her stomach to part her thighs. I wanted to taste her pussy more than I wanted my next breath. She hesitantly spread her thighs for me, and the sight of her juices had me on the edge. I did that to my beautiful mate.

I picked up each leg, kissing the inside of her calves as I put them over my shoulders. She was still looking at me with confusion until I trailed a finger through her slick folds. Her eyes darkened with lust as I rubbed my thumb over her clit and pushed inside her with my index finger. She was so fucking tight. She would need to be well prepped before taking me. That I could do. I thrust my finger in and out, stretching her while her head thrashed back and forth.

"Watch me, precious. Watch me eat this pussy like a starving man." I removed my fingers and licked at the juices that now coated her thighs. Freesia squirmed, trying to get me to that spot where she wanted me most, but I clamped my hands down on her hips.

I licked and sucked and nipped at her until she was screaming my name. A white light burst out of her, practically blinding me as she came all over my tongue. I'd never seen anything like before, but it was the most beautiful thing I'd ever seen. I never wanted it to end, but I could already feel the dream fading. I tried to hold on, but I couldn't. My eyes flashed open, and I felt a very warm, pliant body wrapped around my wolf form. I could feel Freesia's fingers caressing the fur down my flank. Gods, that felt good.

How did you sleep? I startled her with speaking into her mind.

"I had the best dream, but I'm guessing you know that." She giggled and sounded truly happy.

Yes, that was... I trailed off because words couldn't describe how that dream had made me feel.

"Magic." She grinned, and I nodded my wolf's head.

I'm just gonna go shift. I started to move, but she put a hand on me.

"It's not like I didn't just get a full view of you." She giggled.

That was a dream, my love. If I shift in front of you now, I can't be sure we won't finish what we started and solidify the mate bond into something permanent.

I stretched to a stand, then padded to the bathroom. How she had ended up on the floor I had no idea, but I didn't like the fact that I had been so deep in the dream I didn't notice. How was I supposed to protect her if we were so lost in each other in the dream world? I needed to make sure that until the threat had passed, and we were no longer in fear of an abduction, that I would not dream walk with her anymore. It was too much of a risk to her safety.

13

———

FREESIA

I was getting frustrated. Everything in my life was good except for one thing. Weston. It had been weeks since we'd dream walked, and I was pretty sure he was sleeping during the day so he could protect me better at night. He hadn't heard, or felt me move, and honestly, I don't even remember how I made it to the floor and curled around his back. Since then, he wouldn't sleep when I did.

I was making leaps and bounds with my magic. Weston helped me train every morning and always found subtle ways to touch me, but that was it. I was starving for his affection, and it was driving me crazy. He had basically turned to stone. He barely spoke to me unless he was instructing me on my magic. I had only known him for two days before he'd closed himself off. Maybe this was how he always was, or maybe he regretted helping me escape Athos and Baskin. Either way, it put me in a foul mood and temperament the longer it went on.

"How is the training going, princess?" Luka startled me as he walked up behind me.

"Just freaking fine," I grumbled, and he raised his eyebrows in question.

"Trouble in paradise?" He grinned, and I shot him a filthy glare. I was walking through the ice sculptures, trying to find some clarity, but all I could think about was stupid, infuriating Weston and his distance.

"You know he's trying to give you space and his protection. It's the only thing he knows." I looked over at Luka pointedly. I didn't want space or his protection. I wanted him. It was even more obvious after that dream all those weeks ago, but he'd pulled away from me.

"That's not how it feels," I grumbled, seriously not believing I was having that conversation with Luka, who never took anything seriously.

"Tell him that then." He threw his hands up. "You have both been insufferable for the last few weeks. It's really killing my mood. My first few weeks as Alpha should have been fun, but the two of you are a buzzkill." Okay, that was more like the Luka I knew. I chuckled. "Well then, my work here is done. My number one goal was to get you to smile. The storm clouds that have been hanging over us the last few days have been making the wolves restless." He winked as he strolled away.

"Where is he?" I asked Ryker, who had been my ever-present shadow since I arrived.

"I believe he is sleeping so he can keep watch over you tonight, but he specifically said he was not to be disturbed." He bowed his head as if in apology.

"Fine. If he doesn't want to talk to me, that's just fine. Let's go explore the pack's lands. I'm sure there are things I haven't seen still." I tried to brighten my mood, but I couldn't. I wanted to explore with Weston, but he was always too busy sleeping so he could stay up and watch me like a creepy stalker. A thought occurred to me and I grinned. "You know, on second thought, I'm feeling kind of tired after training. I think I may take a nap." Ryker shook his head, but there was a grin on his face.

"That is not wise, princess. West has been increasingly agitated. Best not to interrupt his sleep, but you will see him after he wakes. He guards you every night." He had a point. We were both angry half the time, and I think he was more angry with himself than anyone else.

"Fine. I guess we *are* going exploring then," I growled.

"Princess, I must advise against that as well. I'm your only guard today because Jax and Eli had to take over the perimeter watch to let the other men rest. It is just us today," he said apologetically, and I scowled.

"You don't think that between the two of us we could escape Baskin and Athos?" I raised a brow at him. He reluctantly nodded his consent, and we made our way out to the woods outside the compound. He kept muttering under his breath about stubborn, infuriating princesses, but other than that he followed without complaint.

We walked until the entire area was flooded with tall pines and redwoods. The branches held no leaves because things like that couldn't grow in the blistering cold. I wondered briefly what it felt like to be cold as I danced between the trees. It must not be very pleasant since anytime Molls followed me outside, she would be huddled against me. I knew now why I didn't feel it. Ice ran through my veins.

Ryker kept a short distance from me. I was pretty sure he knew I could use a bit of space right then. I was glad for his intuition, because I definitely wanted some space. Everything in my head was muddled, and I was tired. I wanted Weston, but he was doing his best to avoid me whenever possible. I growled low in my throat. A twig snapped nearby, and I stopped dead in my tracks. Looking behind me, I didn't see Ryker. Had I lost him, or was someone in the woods with us?

"Ryker?" I called, but there was no answer, only the sound of another twig snapping from my other side. "Ryker!" I yelled, trying to alert him to where I was. There was still nothing but silence and clomping feet.

"You ungrateful girl. When we get home, I will remind you what gratitude looks like." I knew that voice and shuddered. They'd brought mother to track me down? No. This wasn't good.

Weston! I screamed inside my head, hoping he would hear me, but there was no response. He'd either blocked me, or he was sleeping so soundly he couldn't hear me.

"I should be grateful to be your prisoner? The girl you basically tortured because you resented me for existing. No. I will not be grateful to you for the way you treated me." My hands tingled as ice coated them. I had been working on my control over the last few weeks and was much better at honing an attack. Where the heck was Ryker? I knew mother was not the only one stalking me.

"Oh, your friend is tied up at the moment." Mother cackled, and my anger grew. What had they done with Ryker? I desperately tried to reach out to Weston again, but there was still no answer. Mother smirked just before something blunt hit me from behind and had pain shooting across my skull. My eyes rolled back in my head as everything went black.

14

———————

WESTON

The dream shifted, and I knew something wasn't right. Freesia was standing in the forest looking at Marlene and about to do something crazy, when Athos came up behind and knocked her unconscious. She cried out for me through our telepathic link, causing my eyes to open and panic to set in. They'd actually come for her. Athos himself had assaulted the princess. Where was Ryker?

What the fuck is going on? I shouted through the link to all my men. They knew better than to leave the princess unprotected. Why had she been alone?

What are you talking about, boss? I just saw the princess less than an hour ago. Luka was genuinely confused. *I told her to talk to you because you have both been insufferable. She didn't come to you?*

I advised Ryker to tell her I was not to be disturbed. Shit.

She must have talked him into taking her exploring. Where the hell are Jax and Eli? My men were all tuned into the link now, waiting for their orders.

Jax spoke up first. *We had to relieve one of the perimeter guys so they could get some rest. Ryker said he would keep her in the gardens and not let her run off into the forest.* I knew the guys were growing attached to my mate, and it made me smile that they were angry something happened to her.

Athos hit her on the head from behind while Marlene taunted her. They are taking her back to their compound by force. We need to hurry before they get back to the wards. I was out the door to my rooms before I even finished my sentence. They would not force my Freesia to do anything she didn't want to do. I would kill them all before I let that happen. *Luka, this is an act of war. Can we stop them from leaving pack lands?*

You want me to declare war on Athos' tribe? Are you sure that's wise, brother? he asked, sounding as uncertain as I felt.

It's probably not, but they took my mate, assaulted her, and are planning to punish her for leaving. I would say those transgressions against the future Queen are enough for the wards to keep them locked in until we can rescue her.

Yes, the wards should recognize the threat. Can you show us where you saw her, so we can go look for her and Ryker? I'm sure our brother did not leave her unattended purposely.

No, he was attacked. I am sure of it. We will find him when we find her. I knew it in my gut that Ryker wouldn't leave her. He'd been the most vocal the last few weeks about the way I'd pulled away from Freesia. He'd thought I was being an asshole, but in reality, I was giving her the time she needed to process everything, without the mate bond breathing down her neck. I'd stopped sleeping when she did to protect her and still failed to do so. Had she called out to me through the link and I hadn't heard her? If she had, I would never forgive myself. *Go, now. I want all of our men out looking for her. Do not come back until she is found,* I barked through the link.

I raced faster than the normal eye could see to the spot where she had been facing off against Marlene. It didn't take a genius to realize the sadistic bitch was the woman she referred to as mother. Her "adoptive mother."

I had never liked Marlene. She always seemed like a snake in the grass, feeding off other people's pain. Now I understood Freesia's need for freedom from that clan. Athos had been corrupted by Marlene. I knew what that crazy bitch was, and I would be damned if I was going to let her harm my mate for even a second longer. I had no idea how she hid her nature from Athos' clan, but I would expose her for what she was.

Be careful, men. Marlene was with her when they took her, I warned. Had I known that was who she called mother, I would have put tighter security on her and stayed with her, even if it meant not sleeping until the threat had passed.

A round of curses filled the link as they all thought about the implications of a crazy Dark Fae infiltrating Athos' clan by marrying the clan leader. This was so much worse than we had thought. I'd thought they would get over it eventually and work toward the greater good, but with one of the most ruthless torturers of the Dark Fae tainting their minds, there was nothing we could do. Marlene wouldn't stop until she had the future Ice Queen under her control. We needed to stop her by any means possible.

I made it to the clearing in a matter of seconds. I could already tell the trail was getting cold. I had wasted too much time talking with my men and I needed action. *Here,* I called through the link, and several of my men popped into existence instantly. It wasn't a power we liked to use around the Snow Wolves. It made them jumpy.

"The trail is going cold. Marlene must have done something to cover her tracks. The princess is in serious danger. The entire clan has been put under her spell," I growled. Half the men shifted to their wolf forms because as a wolf their noses were better. The other half, the ones that were better magic users, rushed off in human form. I closed my eyes, trying to connect with my mate's mind and felt nothing but an inky black block.

"You said Athos knocked her out, right?" Luka strutted up to me, looking pissed.

"Yes," I said. "Why?"

"Even if Marlene blocked her mind, she cannot block her dreams." He shot me a dubious look, and I scowled. Why hadn't I thought of that, and how did he know about the dreams?

"Stay out of my head, Luka. This will be your only warning." I glared at my brother, who chuckled.

"I'm always in your head."

"Fuck off. I need to sleep to see if I can reach her. I need you to watch over my body because our dreams are… intense." I laid on the grass wondering if what I was doing was right. Was I wasting valuable time sleeping so I could dream walk and find her? What if she wasn't dreaming while unconscious? I could lose everything because of my insecurities. I closed my eyes and tried to calm my racing mind. I needed to talk to Freesia right now. Finally, I let sleep claim me and pull me into a dream almost immediately. It was dark and dank. I wondered where my mate's mind had taken her, when I heard Marlene's cackle.

"Poor little Queenie. No one is coming for you. I made sure they would never find our trail. You poor, pathetic girl." I wanted to kill her, but she was only a dream. Nothing I did there would affect the waking world, so even if I killed her there it wouldn't help. I kept to the shadows, making sure not to alert Marlene to my presence. She was a known dream walker who liked to torture people in their nightmares, I needed as much information as I could get. Freesia whimpered, and I spoke into her mind.

It's okay, precious. I'm coming for you. This psycho cannot hurt you, okay. Don't let her know I am here. Let her keep talking until we get enough information to figure out where she is taking you.

Is that really you? She didn't say it out loud, but I heard it softly in my mind, almost like someone was trying to block her, but I still heard her.

Yes, precious. It's me. We are in a dream, at least I think we are. But keep the bitch talking until we figure out where you're going. I will wake up and I will find you, precious. I will always find you.

"What do you want?" Freesia said out loud to Marlene.

"My king will reward me when I bring the Ice Queen to him." She grinned, and I chuckled inside my own head. Her king most definitely would not reward her for bringing the Ice Queen back to the Kingdom. Marlene was delusional. The fastest way to trigger the start of the prophecy was to bring the first princess back to her Kingdom. Azreal would not be impressed that she brought her there instead of killing her, but Marlene's stupidity worked in our favor.

I will come for you, precious. I swear it. I let the dream fade and looked up at Luka, who was staring at me with a puzzled frown.

"She thinks she's taking her to father?" he asked, and I nodded, grinning. No one knew our secret, including a devoted follower of Azreal like Marlene. We could use this advantage to our favor.

"Call the men. It's time to go home." I grinned. Luka didn't look convinced, but he nodded and did as I asked.

"Are you sure about this, brother? She may hate you forever when she finds out the truth."

"At least she will be alive to hate me." I grimaced. I didn't want her to hate me, but if it meant her living through all this, I would do whatever it took to help her. Even if it meant outing myself. Shit. This was going to be bad.

"Okay, brother. I hope you know what you're doing."

Luka shook his head, more serious than he'd ever been. It was why I was the heir. Luka liked messing with people too much. Yes, he could lead the pack, but not the darkness. We had to wait until the time was right, or the Queens would not rise, and darkness would reign. None of us wanted that.

"Let's go home and prepare for an execution." I grinned evilly as Luka helped me to my feet.

"Aye, aye, sire." He pounded his fist against his chest in deference and I shook my head.

"Stop that shit right fucking now. We aren't back home yet, and I will not tolerate it. Get the men together. We need to go." I hated the idea of outing myself to her, but if it saved her from Marlene, then I'd do it. "Let's go save my mate."

15

FREESIA

I woke up slowly, feeling a little better knowing Weston was out there searching for me. I kept my eyes closed. I didn't want mother to know I was awake. I was going to get as much information as I could to give Weston the best chance of saving me. I realized we weren't going to the old compound. We were heading south, not north .

"Oh princess, do you think I believe you are still asleep? You are so completely pathetic. Your mate will not save you. He is a weak hybrid. Azreal will reward me for bringing the first princess to come into her powers to him. You will be consumed, and we will rule over your Kingdom like the rulers we were meant to be." I could practically hear the grin in her voice.

I hated that I ever saw this sadistic creature as my mother. My hands started to ice over, but she was quick to put some cuffs on me and I cried out in pain as whatever metal she had clamped around my wrists sapped my energy. I couldn't make the ice crystals shoot from my palms like Weston had taught me.

"Iron will subdue your magic. Even your little dream walks with the prince. You know Azreal promised him to me if I brought you to him. He will give your mate to me, and you can rest assured that you will be dead before I take my prize," she taunted.

I didn't care. I knew Weston would never let anything happen to me. He was my heart, and I wished I hadn't made him think I needed time. I wanted him more than anything in that moment. I cried out for him in my mind, but everything was silent. He didn't try to reach out to me. My heart shriveled a little that I was alone and powerless against mother.

"You shouldn't have left us, princess. As soon as you started showing signs of magic, we would have taken you to Azreal to be sacrificed for the Dark Fae to rule the Avalon. You would have been revered, but now you will be remembered as the ungrateful girl who refused to sacrifice herself. King Azreal will make you pay for your stubbornness," she growled.

"Fuck off," I breathed through the pain of the cuffs sapping my energy. I hoped that at least if she killed me, she would make it quick.

"The wolf really has corrupted you. What would you think of him if you knew he was the son of the very man who has craved your death? Ohhh, yes, Weston is Azreal's son. His mother was a weak wolf shifter, just like the rest of Azreal's children. I think you know them, no? They have been protecting you for weeks. Don't tell me you didn't know?" Her tinkling laugh made me want to punch her, but all my power was gone because of the iron. I needed to figure a way out of the shackles.

"You really think you can best Weston?" My laugh was cold. I knew I was putting my life in danger, but the woman who had always made me call her mother was completely unhinged. Even with Athos and Baskin under her control, she couldn't stop West from finding me. I had faith in him. He had come for me in my dreams. He would help me. I knew he would. I had the utmost faith in my mate. Holy shit, when had I started thinking about Weston as my mate? He had said I was his, but I hadn't exactly understood what that had meant. Was that why he had distanced himself from me? It made me want to cry. I wouldn't, though. I wouldn't let mother see me lose it. It would make her too happy.

I knew she was a psycho at this point. I knew she only ever cared for her own agenda. Had she made my real mother see her things her way when she betrothed me to Baskin, knowing he would be easily controlled by her? It was entirely possible. The only thing I could do was endure her torture until my mate came to save me, and the longer it took, the harder it was to take.

Don't fret, precious. We will all be there to save you. I know where she is taking you. I will be there. Don't believe your eyes, love, Weston said into my mind. It made me feel so good knowing he was going to be there. I had no idea how he had done it since mother had said she blocked him, but I was grateful.

You will save me from him, won't you, Weston? I almost cried into our link.

The only thing you have to worry about is Marlene and her crazy until we get to you, precious. Don't let her break you. I will give you a sign when the time is right. I love you so much, baby. Don't do anything to make her hurt you, okay? I will be there soon.

I won't, just please hurry, I cried.

What was he doing? Did he have a plan? I couldn't turn anyone to ice with the iron cuffs sapping my energy. He reassured me through the link, and I sighed. Even if I ended up where my crazy adoptive mother wanted to take me, I would still have my mate, and after this was over I would not deny him ever again.

Don't make a vow like that until you see what I am, precious. I love you, and want you more than anything, hold onto that thought until this all gets settled. Just remember that I love you more than anything, please. The desperation in his voice almost made me cry.

I love you too, Weston, please come quickly, I sobbed.

Shhhh, baby, I will be there before you are. Just watch for me, okay? When you see us, even though you think you see monsters, look beneath the surface. I promise you, I will not let Marlene hurt you, my precious princess. I heard the conviction in his voice.

I wondered what he meant about the monsters. He hadn't told me what he was. Was he really a Dark Fae prince as Marlene had suggested? Was he really the enemy? I couldn't think he would have been a part of that. No one had ever told me what the Dark Fae had done to take over the Kingdoms. But if Weston had been a part of the Snow Wolves pack with his men, then they hadn't had a hand in it, right?

My brain was in overdrive as I sat in that cart with my hands cuffed like a common criminal. I had so many questions, but knew I wasn't likely to get any more answers, just more taunts from Marlene. Why had Weston been so cryptic?

It FELT like I had been in that cart for days with Marlene taunting me all the while. She was sick. She told me all the things she was going to do to Weston after I was dead. All it did was fuel my anger. I needed to get these damn cuffs off so I could blast her. I felt my magic just under the surface, but it couldn't manifest because of the cuffs. I had angry, red burns where the metal touched my skin. Marlene has been poking and prodding at them, trying to get me to react. I think it made her more angry when I didn't.

The cart stopped, and Marlene grinned with unrestrained glee. That grin filled me with dread as Athos opened the door and pulled me out roughly. "Are you going to be good, or do I have to knock you out again?"

I glared at him and stood defiantly. I would not hang my

head. They thought they were winning and that they would get their way. I would not walk to my death with anything but the dignity and grace I deserved.

Athos shook his head. "You won't be so smug when the King sees you," he chuckled.

"You were the Queen's most trusted advisor, and you betray her like this?" I scoffed. Athos whirled on me and his meaty fist wrapped around my throat. Wolves I hadn't noticed walking alongside us growled.

"I gave my whole life to her. I did everything for her, and when she needed me the most, she sent me away with an ungrateful little brat. So, yes, I have betrayed her. If she had kept me with her, she might still be here right now." I stared him down even with his hand cutting off my airway.

"You were in love with her," I choked out, and he released me.

"Yes, and I can't stand the sight of you because of it. I'll be glad to be finally rid of you." The words should have hurt, but I was passed caring what these people thought.

I tried to reach out to Weston, but all I got back was silence. My mind started racing. What if something had happened to him? Was he still coming to rescue me, or was I going to have to find a way out of this mess myself?

We stepped up to a beautiful stone archway. It was inlaid with diamonds and sapphires that glowed with magic. The gems were in the shape of snowflakes and the closer we came, the brighter they shone until they were pulsing. The air under the stone arch shimmered like ice crystals, and I grinned. This was home. I could feel the magic in the arch happily welcoming me as if it was excited I was there. I couldn't allow myself to be excited, though, because I was presumably walking to my death.

"After you, princess." Athos bowed with a flourish. It was a mocking bow, and I wanted to punch him, but my hands were still bound. Instead, I held my head high and walked through the portal.

Tingling warmth spread through my veins, and I grinned as the cuffs fell off and hit the frozen ground. I rubbed at my aching wrists as I felt my power rush back into my hands. I almost whirled around to blast Marlene and Athos, but remembered what Weston said. I couldn't give her a reason to hurt me, and I had no idea what kinds of monsters infested my homeland. I knew it was mine though. I could feel it in the trees and the snow and everything around me. The whole place was magical, but something was wrong. They were crying out for me to save them. I didn't know how to do that.

Athos and Marlene came through the portal next, and Marlene shoved me from behind. I stumbled a bit but didn't react except to keep walking forward. Something changed in the land around me. I felt anger spiking. It wasn't my anger, though. Weird. It was like the world around me was angry on my behalf. The trees swayed as a breeze kicked up in a swirling mass. That definitely wasn't me.

Snow and ice pelted the ground around me, and I heard a whisper on the wind. *Run. The trees will guide you.* I was a little startled, but I did what it said. It may have been foolish. I trusted Weston would save me, but that didn't mean I had to make this easy on them. The Ice Kingdom was on my side. I saw it with my own eyes.

Marlene and Athos were cursing as they screamed at me to stop, but I kept going, letting the trees guide me to where I needed to be. I lost them pretty quickly with the storm raging on them and not me. The trees swayed against the wind and I changed direction, hoping that's what it meant when it said the trees would guide me.

I hadn't run for long when the path ended and in front of me was what looked like a cave. The trees swayed toward the opening and I blinked. Maybe I was an idiot for following the movement of the trees, but a cave would be as good a place to hide as any until I figured out what to do next.

16

"Where the fuck is she?" I roared. She should have been there by now. Marlene better not have hurt her, or I would torture her slowly before I killed her.

"We are searching for her, but no one is able to get far because of the ice storm that started so abruptly." Ryker scrubbed a hand over his face.

"Has anyone seen Athos and Marlene?" I growled. I couldn't reach Freesia's mind and it was pissing me off. It was like something was blocking me. I knew it wasn't her because I knew how it felt when she blocked me. This was different, more primal.

"Yes, they found them near the portal, bloody and pelted with ice. The only thing that showed the princess had even been there were a pair of metal cuffs Marlene must have used to block her powers," he sighed.

"She put her in iron?" My rage was palpable. I needed to find her before any of the other creatures of the Dark Court did. I would deal with Marlene and Athos as soon as I found my mate. I took a couple deep breaths to cool my temper. She was in danger and I needed to stay calm if I was going to save her. "When did this freak ice storm start?" I asked thoughtfully.

"Athos was blubbering like a baby when they found him," Luka chuckled as he walked into the throne room. "He said the princess started the storm and ran away into the trees."

"She didn't start the storm," I grumbled. "The land is responding to her. Did he say what happened before the storm hit?" I had an idea, but I needed confirmation.

"He said they walked through the portal. Marlene shoved her to get her moving, then wind and ice pelted everywhere except for where the princess stood." He shrugged. "Sounds like she caused it to me." He was way too happy to be in my presence. I needed to get out of there to search for her myself, but the royal guards had made it clear I was not to leave the palace. I was too important to their plans. Azreal wanted me contained. I was his heir, and he believed me to be loyal, even though I'd left before the carnage in the snow Kingdom had started. I refused to help him slaughter innocents just because he wanted the Kingdoms for his own. He was on a path of destruction I wanted no part of.

As if merely thinking of the demon conjured him, Azreal

walked into the room with a flourish. "My sons, so good to have you home." His grin made my skin crawl. I'd spent the last eighteen years away from him, and it hadn't been long enough.

"Father," I gritted out as I bowed.

"It is fortunate you came now. The sacrifice is on the way, and we will rule the Kingdoms together."

"That is very fortunate father," Luka stepped in before I could say something we would all regret later. "But it seems the incompetent wretch you sent to retrieve her has lost her yet again." Why on earth had he told him that? I was seriously going to kill Luka if anything happened to her.

"She what?" he roared. His face turned purple as he appeared to grow. Shit, this was bad.

"Father," Luka sighed. "Let us go search for the lost princess. We will bring her back for you." I kept my eyes from widening as I realized what an evil mastermind Luka was. He was giving me the opportunity I needed to leave to go find her without making father suspicious.

"Yes, father. We will go find the missing princess and bring her back for the sacrifice." The words tasted like acid on my tongue, but I needed him to believe we were on his side. He calmed, and I nearly breathed a sigh of relief. I wasn't ready to kill him yet, but I would need to be soon. I just had to wait until the time was right.

"Very well," he growled. "Go and bring back the girl." He looked me hard in the eyes, like he could somehow see the deception. I lowered my eyes and bowed to him, even though

I wanted to shove my obsidian blades through his heart. *Soon.*

"You heard the king. We leave at once to find the princess." I ordered. All my brothers put their fists over their hearts as we left the throne room. I guess killing Luka would have to wait for another day. As always, he appeared to have concocted a devious plan and I couldn't wait to hear what he had cooked up.

17

FREESIA

I spent the night at the back of the cave trying to figure out what I was going to do next. I fell asleep for a while but had no dreams. Where was Weston? Was he looking for me at all? Did he even know I was gone? Something poked me in the ribs, and I sat up with my hands at the ready to defend myself against whatever threat was there. I was a little groggy still, but whatever it was I had never seen before, a tiny little man with wings and a little bronze sword. "Did you stab me with that?" I noticed a small amount of blood on the top of the sword and the creature grinned.

"Who are you?" the creature grumbled, looking around. He sniffed the blood on the end of his sword and to my horror licked it clean.

"My name is Freesia. What are you?" I asked as I backed away from the bloodthirsty thing.

"Freesia? The Ice Princess? We have been waiting for you, Your Highness." His little dragonfly wings fluttered as he bowed in midair. He almost over corrected into a somersault, but caught himself just in time.

"Yes, that's me. Please don't bow. I'm not much of a princess right now. I'm running from a crazy lady who wants to sacrifice me to the Gods, or something equally insane." I scrubbed a hand over my face. Was I dreaming? I'd never remembered having any dreams other than the one with Weston, but maybe I had finally cracked? "You never told me what you are."

"I'm a blood sprite, Highness. Please come with me. The others will be so excited you're finally here. Did the trees lead you to us?" I nodded and had found myself being led by a blood sprite who stabbed me then drank my blood to who knows where. And that even wasn't the weirdest thing that had happened to me in the last few weeks.

I followed the little bloodsucker to the cave wall and shot him a dubious look. He knocked three times in an intricate pattern, and the wall to the cave opened up into a huge cavern. I looked around in awe at the space and the hundreds of different creatures moving around. "What is this place?" I breathed.

"We are what is left of the true Court of Ice, Highness. We have been here protecting the crown until your return," the little man said.

"I'm sorry, I didn't get your name." He blinked and then his cheeks pinked.

"You can call me Barty, Highness. That's what everyone calls me." He ducked his head, and I grinned.

"Well, Barty. No more of this Highness business. I just want to be called Freesia, okay?" I raised a brow at the little man, and he nodded.

"Yes, High–I mean Freesia." It sounded like it almost pained him to say my name, and I wondered if I should have just let him continue with the formalities. "I must take you to the council. They will be most excited to see you," he chirped and sped off. I guessed I was meant to follow, so I did. He was a fast little thing as he weaved between numerous creatures I'd never even imagined were real. I had a hard time keeping up because of the crowd.

"Barty, wait. I can't move through crowds like you," I huffed. He came whizzing back to perch on my shoulder.

"Right, mages are a bit more clunky than a sprite," he agreed, like he was the one who knew it all along. I rolled my eyes at the little sprite as he directed me where to go.

"What is a mage?" I asked because I still knew so little about this world.

"A magic user. Your mother Queen Hypernia was the most powerful mage in all the Kingdoms, but she ruled with kindness. She never expected a war to break out with the Dark Fae until the prophecy came to light. She thought she could negotiate with Azreal, but by that time it was too late and the only thing she could do to preserve the land was send you away. How did you get home? Did Athos bring you back? Where is your betrothed?" The little man just knew how to twist the knife.

"Athos and Baskin are traitors. Athos hit me over the head and was going to deliver me to Azreal to be sacrificed. He, along with Marlene and Baskin, cannot be trusted," I growled. In the end they had done me a favor, though. They had reunited me with my people.

We came to a huge set of double doors made completely of ice, and the sprite shivered. "You feel cold?" I asked with a raised brow.

"Y-yes, the ice Kingdom is not really my home. Many of us have fled into caves and the underground. This is the Ice Council chambers. They will see that you are taken care of," he said before flying away. That wasn't exactly comforting. He didn't even tell me what to do. Was I supposed to knock, or were they expecting me? I hadn't a clue, so I erred on the side of politeness and knocked.

"Enter," a loud, disembodied voice bellowed from the other side of the door. I shrugged and pushed it open. Three creatures sat at a table looking at me with a mixture of awe and suspicion. The man in the middle had long silver hair down to his waist, and his eyes were the same blue-violet as mine. His features were sharper, but it was almost like looking in a distorted mirror. "What is your name, child?" he asked much more softly this time. I was mesmerized by the face in front of me.

"My name is Freesia," I said softly. The stupid sprite should have come with me. Little chicken.

"Freesia, and how did you get here?" he asked, raising a brow. I told him the story about being taken from the wolves' compound and brought to the Ice Kingdom, only to be rescued by a crazy ice storm and trees that showed me the way to a cave where I ran into Barty who brought me there. They listened to the story, but not one of them showed a flicker of emotion on their face as I finished, spreading my hands out in front of me. "How did you come to be with wolves?"

"Weston of the Snow Wolves pack came to my room at the compound injured. I cleaned his wounds, then we were attacked by bears. Athos blamed me for everything, so I ran away. I was tired of being caged like an animal. I just wanted to be free." I sighed.

"Weston is not of the Snow Wolves pack. He is the Dark Heir and not to be trusted," the man growled. His eyes like glaciers as he glared at me.

"Cut the crap, Malcom. We can all see you know she is who she says she is, and that boy left his father long before the carnage started. He helped get many of our innocents out before the war began," the woman next to him said. She had stick straight hair the color of moonbeams, and her eyes were the same as Malcom's.

"Do I know you? You both look so familiar to me." I clenched and unclenched my fists, hoping I had enough control that a dagger wouldn't appear. I looked down and was happy to see none did.

"Dear one, that is because I am your grandmother and this brooding idiot is my son, your father." I'd known it from the second I saw him, but having it confirmed caused me to stumble back. The woman stood and wrapped a comforting arm around me as she led me to a chair.

"You don't look old enough to be a grandmother," I said absently.

A tinkling laugh left her lips. "Thank you. We live very long lives and stop aging around twenty-five. Has no one told you of your heritage? Your people?" When I shook my head, she tsked.

"That is unfortunate. Your mother would have wanted you to know what was to come." She sighed.

"Freesia?" Malcom said softly in almost a reverent tone. "You really are here. We'd hoped that sending you away with Athos would keep you safe from the war this world faced." He put his head in his hands.

"Athos betrayed us because he was in love with my mother and resented me for him being sent away. He thought if he was here, he would have been able to save her." I had no idea if that was his delusion or the truth, but I knew he hated me enough to turn me over to a monster because of it.

"That might have been true, but the prophecy was clear that the four baby princesses would be the ones to take back from the dark. We did what had to be done, and Athos took you to that frozen wasteland gladly. I'm truly sorry he mistreated you. If we had known he would turn bitter, we would have chosen someone else."

"It's fine," I grumbled. "I know everyone did what they

thought was best. All that matters now is that we take down the evil king."

"It won't be easy, Freesia." Malcom sighed. "We have been trying to think of ways to keep you out of this fight for years. All the creatures here have built our own underground home away from the dark influence of the king. I think we should stay hidden until the rest of the princesses are recovered." He scrubbed a hand over his face.

"With all due respect, I can't do that. The Kingdom is crying out for me to help it. The trees and the wind and even the earth are begging me to stop the onslaught. They helped me get away from Marlene and Athos. I owe it to the land and the people to stand up and fight," I growled. Tingles traveled up my arms and something weighed heavy on my head. Reaching up, I noticed a crown now sat on my head. It wasn't the weirdest thing I'd ever experienced, but it still freaked me out a bit. "What? How?" I cried as I tried to take it off, but it wouldn't budge.

"The crown decides if you're worthy to lead, little one. You are the heir, but only in name until the crown decides if you are worthy. It has decided. You are the Queen, and we will go to battle if that is what you wish." Malcom's eyes sparkled with pride as he said the words.

Holy crap. What had I gotten myself into?

18

WESTON

I could always feel the land in this realm like a living, breathing entity, but this was different. Something had happened recently, and the land was rejoicing. I had an idea that it had something to do with my princess. She was somewhere nearby or had been close not too long ago.

"Do you feel that?" I asked Luka and Ryker. They both nodded. "Something has happened. Something has changed," I grumbled.

"Freesia came home to save the realm from our tyrant father. I'd say that is enough of a reason for the land to be excited, but where is she?" Ryker asked softly.

We had gone to the portal, noting that the storm had stopped, then made our way through the trees, but we couldn't find her and the longer we walked, the more lost we became, like we were purposely being led in circles.

"I'm going to try something," I groaned because I knew I would look like a lunatic. "Don't fucking say a word." I glared at them all. They looked away as I walked to the nearest tree and leaned my hands and forehead on its trunk. *I just need to find her to make sure she is safe.* I spoke in my mind and pushed the words at the tree. I could hear my brothers snickering but used our link to send them a mental fuck you. This had to work.

Why? a voice whispered on the wind.

Read my intentions. I'm an open book. She is my mate and the only thing I wish is to see her happy. I replied to the tree and let my mental barriers down. I didn't care how stupid I looked or what it took to get some help in locating her. All I cared about was finding her and defeating my father once and for all.

She has been crowned. Do you think she will still want you when she sees what you really are? the tree asked softly.

It doesn't matter if she wants me as long as she is safe and protected. I will gladly leave her alone if that is her wish. I let the tree see the band around my heart. The vow I'd made not to push her into mating. The tree hummed in approval.

You truly love the new Queen? it asked.

Yes, more than my own life. More than the lives of my brothers, who would go to war to help me. More than any realm. I love her with every part of me. If she doesn't want me, that is fine. I will walk away. It will cost me the very breath in my lungs to do so.

Yes, I see your devotion. We sent her to the underground. Watch the trees. They will guide you.

Thank you, Goddess Earth. I knew that was who it was. The entity I was speaking to. It was the only entity who could speak through the trees.

You are welcome, Weston. I hope you get the Queen to see what I do. I know she cares. Just show her your heart. Goddess Earth said, and then there was nothing.

"Are you done making out with trees yet?" Luka chuckled and I flipped him off.

"I was speaking with Goddess Earth, you jackass." His eyes widened at my words and he shut his smirking mouth.

"We need to follow the trees to the underground. Watch the branches and let me know if they sway a certain way or change direction." They nodded, and we started walking. I was keeping my senses trained on my surroundings as the others directed me on what the trees were doing. They were actually leading us somewhere. I just hoped they weren't leading us off a cliff.

We wandered like that for some time until we came to the mouth of a cave. I wondered how the underground survived in such a small dark space, but figured they'd probably used magic to make a place big enough for them to hide in. I stepped forward, but Ryker put a hand on my arm. "Let me go first. It could be a trap."

"You really think a Goddess would lead us into a trap? She read my intentions. She knows how I feel about my mate. She would not lead us into a trap," I growled.

"Humor me. You are the future of our race. I do not want to leave anything to chance." I took a step back with wide eyes, not fully understanding what he was saying. I was absolutely not the future of our race. I was the heir, but I didn't deal with the Dark Court the way my father did. He was ruthless and cruel. I'd need to be that as well if I planned to be the king of the dark. The creatures saw anything less as weakness.

"Fine, go, but do not call me that again. I will be king, yes, but I refuse to lead the way he does." I glared at Ryker, who nodded. He walked inside the cave and minutes went by before I heard him curse and come running out of the cave with something small flying around his head. It looked like a sprite, but I hadn't seen one in years that wasn't locked in the king's dungeon. He was a vicious little thing with a bronze sword that he used to try to stab Ryker in the eyes. I couldn't help the loud laugh that left me as Ryker, the big bad Dark Fae, cursed and batted at the thing.

I grabbed the wings of the sprite in a motion quicker than the eye could see and held it away from me. His little sword slashed up and a small line the size of a paper cut bloomed on my wrist. I winced but didn't make a noise. "We are not your enemy, little sprite. Goddess Earth led us here so I could find my mate and help her fulfill her destiny." I shot him a pointed look.

"Prove it. You are Dark Fae and known deceivers," he spat at me, swinging his blade again for good measure.

"I am also wolf. As are my brothers. My mother was of the

Snow Wolves, the most fierce protectors of the Queen. Luka is now their Alpha." I nodded to Luka, who grinned.

"You lie. He is not a snow wolf. He cannot be Alpha." The sprite glared at me, swinging clumsily again, trying to get away.

"I challenged their Alpha and won, little maggot. It doesn't matter which pack you hail from if you win the Alpha challenge." Luka stepped forward threateningly. I held up a hand to calm him. We weren't trying to start small battles with blood sprites. We were much stronger than them.

"Look at the trees, little sprite. Are they not showing us where to go?" He looked unsure but took a look at the tall pines where it looked like fingers were pointing to the cave as they swayed in that direction.

"The council will not like this," he said in a small voice. "You promise not to hurt the Queen?"

"I could never hurt the Queen. She is my mate. I love her more than my own life. Lead the way, little sprite." I let go of his wings and he sped off into the cave. We followed close behind, and I memorized the series of knocks he made to open the cavern. I knew it may come in handy one day. Even if we freed the Ice Court, the others wouldn't be able to live there until the other Courts were restored. We would need a way to help them get supplies and information.

The wall opened into a cavern, and what sounded like a celebration could be heard. I was nervous. I didn't always look the same in this realm, and I wondered what Freesia would see. Would she see the monster or the man? I hoped it was the latter because I didn't ever want to see her look at me with fear. "Stay here, Master Weston. I need to let the Queen know you are here." The sprite bowed.

"She already knows," Luka said softly as he pointed to a small stage. My princess stood there in a gown so pale blue it almost looked white. Her blue-violet eyes shone with happiness as she looked up at me, and I exhaled a relieved breath. She didn't see the monster hiding under the surface. She saw the man.

Weston, she called out in my head. *Is that you? You look so different here.*

It's me, precious. I told you I would find you. She started to move toward me, but a hand came down on her shoulder, halting her. Malcom. I'd known he was her father the minute I laid eyes on her, and the elf was not my biggest fan. I growled low in my throat as he spoke quietly in her ear. Freesia scowled and shrugged him off.

I practically ran through the crowd to get to her and pulled her into my arms as she leaped for me. I didn't care about the gasps of any of the creatures in the room. It had been too long since I'd held my precious princess in my arms.

"I'm actually a Queen now." She shrugged. "The crown chose me or something."

"It couldn't have chosen anyone more deserving, my love." I kissed her hard. I tried to keep my fangs from elongating, but it was impossible with her beautiful body pressed against mine. Breaking the kiss, I rested my forehead against hers. "I have a plan. Do you trust me?" I needed the answer because this plan was so crazy, I was going to need complete faith to pull it off.

"I have a plan too." She grinned. "We are going to take my Kingdom back." She had so much confidence that it had a sense of pride filling me.

"We are, my love. Let's go talk and maybe we can combine our plans into one." I wrapped my arms around her. I couldn't believe she was actually there, and she looked so gorgeous in that gown with her crown of ice on top of her head.

"Later, there is something else we need to do first." She winked and pulled me away from the crowd. It was only seconds before Malcom snatched her arm. I growled low in warning. I knew he was her father, but if he didn't take his hand off her, I would remove it completely.

"Calm yourself, mutt." His haughty tone pissed me off. "Freesia. You don't see the monster along with the man?" He pointed at me, and I wanted to choke him where he stood.

"No Malcom, I see the kind, loving man who made my happiness his priority and promised to protect me for eternity. I don't need to know what species he is to know that he loves me, and that I love him back. He is mine and you don't get to take that from me," she growled.

"Fine. If you can't see the monsters we all see when we look at them, then maybe there is something redeemable in him," he huffed.

"Malcom, I already told you to stop being so hard on Weston. He helped get innocents out of the realm when his father first started the campaign against us. He is not our enemy." Gwendolyn, Malcom's mother, yelled from down the hall. I was pretty sure every creature in the cavern had heard her reprimand her son, and his eyes glowed with rage.

"Thank you, Gwen, for such kind words." I ducked my head at the older woman, and she smiled.

"It doesn't mean he is good enough for my daughter." Malcom raged. Freesia ripped her arm from his grasp and took a step closer to me.

"You don't get to decide that. I do. The only father figure I ever knew betrayed me. So, excuse me if I don't want to take your advice. The only person who has been true to me in my life is Weston," she yelled.

"I take offense to that," Luka joked.

"Shut the fuck up, Luka. I'm making a point here," she chuckled and rolled her eyes, and Luka winked at her. I knew he was trying to dissolve the tension. "I'm going to my rooms with my mate. If you don't like that, well, too damn bad. I am my own person and I want Weston. We will fight for the King-doms together, and we will win." She pulled me away from the gawking crowd. I had a goofy smile on my face. I was so fucking proud. She would make a fierce Queen. And I was so glad she chose me to share that with.

She pulled me along until we were away from everyone and I grabbed her hips, pulling her into my body. "You are so sexy when you take charge," I breathed against her ear. She shivered. "I was lost without you, precious. I'm sorry I shut you out. I thought it was the only way to protect you."

"Weston, shut up until we get to my room." She giggled when I growled.

"Lead the way, my love." I really couldn't wait to see what she had planned once we got to her room.

We came to a door, and she smiled at me over her shoulder. "I missed you so much. The last few weeks have been hell."

"You have no idea, my love. I wish I hadn't put so much distance between us. It nearly killed me when I realized after everything I'd done to protect you that you were still brought here to act as a sacrifice." I sighed. She looked up at me with watery eyes.

"I know you thought what you were doing was for the best, but it did hurt. I shouldn't have left the compound, though. I should have listened to Ryker and not gone exploring. I wanted to visit you in your dreams, but Ryker said that would be a bad idea." She looked away and my hands came up to cup her cheeks.

"I will never hold myself away from you again, my love. I'm so sorry I hurt you. I will spend the rest of my life making it up to you," I breathed as I dipped my head to her lips. I couldn't hold myself back a second longer. She turned the handle on the huge door, backing inside with a smile.

"Close the door?" she asked as she removed the ice crown from her head. I watched in awe as she started unlacing the corset of her dress as she looked at me with a sexy smile. "Are you just going to stand there, or are you going to help me out of this?"

"I don't want to shred it with my teeth and scare you, precious." Her smile turned devious.

"Maybe I want to see your savage side." She smirked. I couldn't stop myself from lunging for her and wrapping my arms around her waist.

"Be careful what you wish for, my love." My smile was feral as I stalked toward her. "Unlace it, quickly. This dress looks too beautiful on you for me to ruin it." I clenched my clawed fists at my sides. I wanted to shred the dress from her body and just have another one made. She quickly unlaced the corset, and I watched as she slowly slid the dress down her body. "Are you sure? We don't have to do this if you're not ready." It would kill me to walk out of that room. I would love nothing more than to act out the dream, but I needed her to be sure.

"Weston, no more hiding. I want to be yours and make you mine." Her eyes glistened as she let the material slide to the floor, leaving her completely naked. She was even more beautiful than she had been in the dream. I couldn't stop myself from moving to her if I had wanted to, which I didn't. I grabbed her bare waist and made my clothes disappear with my mind.

"I thought that was something you could only do in dreams," she groaned.

"I never said that, love. I'm more powerful than most, but is this what you want to talk about right now?" I asked as I dipped my head to her nipple and rolled my tongue around it.

"Oh Gods, no. Weston. I need you so bad," she practically yelled.

"Shhhh, love, they are already going to be talking." I chuckled as I moved my mouth to her other nipple and gave it the same treatment.

"Let them fucking talk," she growled. "I don't care. I want you now and forever, Weston. Do what you said. Mark me in every way. I'm yours." My eyebrows raised as she looked down at me where I was licking at her nipples.

"I am yours as well, for eternity," I vowed, and I felt the mating bond wrap around my heart. I picked her up and moved her to the bed. I would make her come over and over before I marked her because the mark would make the orgasm that much more pleasurable for both of us.

I laid her out on the bed and looked down at her porcelain skin. She was exquisite in every way. I pushed her thighs apart, grinning. I hadn't forgotten how tight she was. I could never forget that dream. I licked across her breasts as my fingers made their way down her belly to her center. "I need to get you ready, baby. I won't fit if I don't, and I want to fuck you all night long."

"Yesss, do whatever you want to me Weston, I am yours," she breathed as I shoved one finger inside her core and cursed. She was already clenching against me in anticipation.

"Easy, baby. Relax. I want to make you feel good. I wanna make you come so many times you forget your own name before I sink my teeth into you and make you mine." I knew this was a bad idea, but I couldn't stop myself from doing it. If

I failed to save her, at least I would go into the afterlife with her. A true mating bond meant that if one died the other did as well, which was just as well because if she died I would not want to live another second.

She stopped squeezing my finger as I pushed in and out of her. My tongue laved at her nipple as she thrashed her head back and forth. "You like that, sexy. I'm going to make you come so many times you don't remember your own name, but you will be screaming mine," I whispered against her breast as I thrust a second finger inside her tight pussy. "Gods, precious. I don't know if I'm gonna fit if you don't come soon." I thrust my fingers in and out, scissoring them to stretch her before I started kissing down her stomach. I would make her come on my fingers before I licked her juices up with my tongue. I curled my fingers, touching that spot that had her entire body bowing off the bed as she screamed.

"Good girl. Now the fun can really begin. Watch me, beautiful. I want you to see the way I devour you. Your orgasms are mine, and mine alone." I picked her legs up and slung them over my shoulders. She would come even harder on my tongue. I would make sure of it. I grinned at her dazed look before I flattened my tongue and slid it up her slit. Her moan and the taste of her had me almost to the brink of my control. My cock was rock hard, but this wasn't about me. This was about my perfect mate. I looked up at her. Her head was tilted and her back was arched as I licked and sucked at her clit. She moaned, her hands fisting my hair to hold me to her pussy. Gods, she was absolutely divine.

"Weston, I need you, please," she yelled, and I couldn't hold myself back any longer. I attacked her pussy until she came again and licked up every bit of her juices. She screamed as she came, and I lapped at her until she came down from her second orgasm.

"I'm gonna fuck you now. Feel free to scream for me now because when you come, I will make you mine forever. There's no stopping if we continue, baby. Tell me now if you don't want it," I said, but hoped she didn't tell me no. I couldn't handle it if she didn't want to be mine.

"Make me yours forever, Weston. I love you so much. I want to be with you for eternity." The words from her mouth had both sides of me growling. Flipping her over so her ass was in the air, I gripped her hips and licked at the pulse point in her neck. I was practically feral as she moaned. My fingers once again found her folds and pushed in and out. "Fuck. Weston, please. I need you. Not your fingers, you," she groaned. I couldn't deny her request as I lined my cock up to her entrance. She was on all fours, swaying her ass in my face, and the only thing I could do was grab her hips to hold her still.

"For someone innocent, you are so sexy and wanton." I rubbed my cock on her pussy. I wanted confirmation that she wanted me. For someone of my status, I felt self-conscious with this beautiful girl. She shifted her hips to get the part of me inside her that she craved.

"Fuck, Weston. Please," she moaned again as she wiggled her hips. I'd pressed my tip against her opening, but I had to stop because I was going to lose it before she got to come again.

"Baby, please. I'm holding myself back as much as I can, but if you keep begging I won't be able to stop myself."

"Then don't. Fuck me, Weston. I already told you to make me yours." She grinned over her shoulder. I couldn't stop myself from giving in to her commands. She was my heart, and I would give her whatever she wanted. I pushed my aching cock into her, and my eyes closed. She was the most exquisite woman in the realms, and I could not think of anything but claiming her.

I drove in and out of her tight pussy until she winced, and I forced myself to stop. Shit. She had been a virgin until now. Even as I pushed my fingers inside her, I hadn't felt the barrier.

"Are you okay, my love? We can stop if it hurts too bad," I breathed against her neck.

"Do not stop. Please, Weston. Please don't stop," she whimpered, and I couldn't stop myself from giving her what she needed. I pushed into her roughly as I fingered her clit and her neck arched, almost as if she knew what I needed to connect us for eternity. I licked up the side of her neck as I pistoned my hips in and out of her. She felt so incredible and my fangs elongated.

"Are you sure you want this, my love?" I gave her one last out. She shook her head and pushed her ass into my cock, causing me to slide even further inside of her. She felt like heaven, and I wanted to claim her in every sense of the word.

I fucked her hard, and she cried out as my fangs bit into her neck. The second they broke the skin, the endorphins pulsed through me. It made everything in my body light up like it never had before. I felt her lifeblood flow into my mouth, causing me to come uncontrollably inside Freesia as she screamed my name. I felt our minds meld together. She was now mine, and I was hers. I licked the skin that I had broken at her throat when I had marked her. "You're mine now. No one will ever take you from me," I said as I kissed her lips and we both fell asleep.

19

I was completely sated as I looked up at Weston with the utmost love in my eyes. "What did we do? Is this going to put you in danger?" After everything we had been through, I knew the vow he'd made to me could put his life in danger.

"No. I have a plan, my love. He will not risk his only heir," he said with confidence, but it didn't make me feel better.

"Weston. This is not okay. We are now linked. I wouldn't change it for the world, but what about Azreal? He hates my kind enough to cause mass genocide among my people. How do we stop that?" I asked as laid in his arms.

"I have a plan, my love. Trust me." He looked at me with pleading eyes.

"Of course. What are we doing?" I asked, not knowing exactly what was going to happen.

"I'm sorry, my love. I have to take you to Azreal to give him a false sense of security before I challenge him. I promise you I will win, and you will be safe.

"Wait? You are going to challenge the Dark Fae king?" I yelled. I didn't like that Weston had to challenge his father. I hated it. I didn't want him to have that worry. I wanted to be with him forever, and I didn't want him to have to kill his father for that to happen.

"I will challenge anyone who threatens you, my love. Including my father, who decided to take over your realm without any provocation." He kissed my forehead.

"Babe, I need to know that this world is worth saving, are you the only one I can trust?" I asked

Weston with pleading eyes. He pulled me close to his naked body, and I moaned against him.

"No, my men are also my brothers. They are as trustworthy as I am," he said as he kissed my temple. "Luka and Ryker love you almost as much as I do." He smiled at me.

"They do not," I chuckled. Luka and Ryker were only there because of Weston. They didn't care about me.

"They do. Not as much as I love you, but they have been searching for you as hard as I have, love." Weston made me feel like an asshole.

"Don't feel like that, baby," he said.

"I love you, too, so much. How do we stop your father?" I asked.

"I will worry about him. All you have to do is be there. You don't need to be involved in that." He kissed my shoulder where he had marked me. I could feel his mark inside and out. We were connected in every way, and if he had to take me to Azreal for this war to be over, then so be it. He'd taken over my realm and my people, but I would fight if he thought to take Weston from me. I would not let him lose. A fierce determination rose up inside of me.

"Defeating Azreal will make you the king of the Dark Fae, right?" I asked because I knew he didn't want that.

"It's worth it, precious. To make sure you're safe, I would defeat a thousand dictators. I don't want you to ever feel unsafe." He kissed the mark again and it pulsed, making me feel his utmost devotion to me. I moaned, pushing against him. "Love, if you keep doing that, we won't get any sleep, and going into battle without sleep is a bad idea." I pouted as I looked up at him. He chuckled as he kissed me. "I promise you, precious, we will have all the time in the world for that once I defeat my father." He kissed my lips again, and I couldn't help but grind against him. He cursed, and I grinned. "I think I have created a monster," he chuckled.

"Yes, yes, you have, and I want more, now," I groaned as he slid his fingers between my folds and started circling my clit. It was heaven, but not what I really wanted. Reaching down, I grabbed his huge cock in my hand and pumped it. I watched as his eyes went dark, and he rolled on top of me, putting his weight on his elbow so he didn't crush me. The fingers that had just been on my clit went to his mouth, and he sucked my desire from them, closing his eyes and moaning. My hand was still wrapped around him, and I pumped harder until he groaned and moved my hands above my head. He caged both my hands in one of his as his eyes slowly moved down my body to the place where I was aching for him.

"Well, I guess if you are demanding more, it wouldn't be right to deny my mate what she wants." He slid down my body achingly slow, and it only heightened the anticipation of what he was going to do next. He licked at my inner thighs as he pushed two fingers inside me, and my back arched. This was the most exquisite torture. My hands fisted in his hair as he continued torturing me slowly with just his skilled fingers. "I'm gonna mark you, here." He nipped at my inner thigh and my head thrashed.

"Oh, Gods, yes," I moaned. I wanted him to mark me to my very soul. I could feel in his mind how turned on he was, and it just made my body go crazy. I bucked against his fingers and just as white-hot pleasure burned through me, I felt his claiming bite on my thigh. My vision went black for a second, and I screamed louder than I ever had before.

As the haze lifted, Weston crawled back up my body, kissing a path as he went until he pushed his erection inside of me again. Gods, he felt so good. "I don't think I can come again," I breathed, but Weston just chuckled as he thrust harder.

"You can and you will, little mate." His grin was mischievous. His lips pressed against the mating mark on my neck and the sensation had me climbing to the peak again. "That's it, baby. Feel that? We are perfect together. You see me when all everyone else sees is a monster." He kissed the mark again. "Come for me, now." My body responded instantly to his command, and my walls squeezed him as he thrust a few more times before he came on a grunt, then collapsed next to me and pulled me into his arms. "Sleep, precious. It may be our last bit of peace for a while."

20

WESTON

Freesia fell asleep within minutes, but I couldn't get sleep to come. My mind whirled with what I had to do. I had to place the thing I held most dear in the direct path of a tyrant. I didn't want her anywhere near my father and his minions, but how else was I supposed to get the upper hand?

Stop thinking so loud, you're giving me a damn headache, Luka said through the link.

Fuck off, I growled back.

The plan is sound. Don't worry. We won't let anything happen to her while you are fighting the old man.

I don't even want her in the same room as him.

None of us want to bring her there, but the best way to distract him is to make him think he's won. We need that false sense of security to use to our advantage, he reminded me. I knew what the stakes were, and I knew this was the best chance for our survival, but it still bothered me. I hated the idea of bringing her there.

I know the stakes, Luka. I will not deviate from the plan. I groaned. I knew the consequences if I didn't do this. We would be hunted down and slaughtered. There was only one way this would work, and that was if I took her into the den of the beast.

Okay, we should go soon. Azreal will start to wonder what's taking us so long and send out a search party. And we absolutely do not want that. He was right. We didn't want the hounds coming for our scents because they would destroy everything, and everyone in the underground. Once Freesia was Queen, we would let everyone go back to their homes to rebuild. There would be no need for the underground.

Yes, I just want to let her sleep for a bit before we go start facing monsters.

Not too long. He's gonna get restless soon, Ryker popped in. Oh, great, it was a fucking party.

I know, okay? Gods. I just want to give her some time to rest. I shook my head even though the dicks couldn't see me and nuzzled Freesia's neck as I tried to wake her up. It had only been a couple hours since she'd fallen asleep, but we all knew we had a small window before our actions put everyone in the underground in danger. Freesia whimpered as if she was scared, and it made me wonder what the fuck she was dreaming about. It sounded a lot like fear. Had Azreal gotten to her in her dreams, or had he sent one of his dream walkers to mess with her?

"Wake up, precious." I shook her until her eyes popped open wide in terror. "Freesia, my love, are you okay?" She looked at me with confusion for a second before a look of relief passed over her face.

"I had the most awful dream," she cried. "You can't challenge your father, Weston. You can't." She was holding on to me with desperate hands and sobbing as she pressed her face into my chest.

"Shit, his dream walkers were in your dreams. They know part of the plan." I scrubbed a hand through my hair. I didn't know what to do, so I reached out to Luka and Ryker through the link.

We need a new plan. His dream walkers were just torturing Freesia, I growled.

This is the only plan that has any chance of succeeding, West, Luka said softly. *I have seen it, West. The only way this works is with the plan we have in place. Trust me. It's the only way.* He was serious, and I reluctantly nodded even though he couldn't see me. I was sure he could feel my agreement.

"What is it?" Freesia asked with wide eyes.

"Nothing, precious. The plan stays the same. We need to go before Azreal sends his bloodhounds and they track us to the underground."

"We can't let that happen," she gasped, eyes alert as she jumped from the bed to find her clothes. "We have to go, now." She sounded so regal as she worried about her people.

Pride swelled in my chest as I watched her. "What are you waiting for, West? We need to go. They can't find this place," she cried. I waved a hand, and we were both dressed. "You could do that this whole time? We are wasting time. We need to lead the assassins away from here." She stomped her foot.

"We will make sure they don't find the underground, love, but we need to leave now." I pulled her toward the door. I didn't like that he'd had his dream walkers tracking her.

As soon as we got to the main meeting room, my men, my brothers, were standing at attention waiting for us. I looked at them, knowing I may not see them again after this day. I might not see anyone ever again if Azreal was able to defeat me in my challenge, but I knew we could destroy him if everything went to plan.

"We need to get out of here. Once we free the Ice Kingdom, they will be able to go home and rebuild their lives," I said loudly to all the creatures that were still mulling around. "We will be back for you once we defeat Azreal," I declared. A cheer went through the crowd. I grinned as I looked at Freesia. She had her crown on and was smiling. I looked in confusion, not remembering her putting the crown on before we came out of the bedroom. "Did you put that on before we left the room?" My eyes moved to the top of her head and her eyes widened.

"Umm, no. It likes to just appear sometimes." She reached up to take it off but couldn't. "It seems to want to show Azreal who the real ruler is," she sighed. "This isn't good."

"It will be fine, precious." I pulled her close, even

though I wasn't as confident as I sounded. If Azreal and his people saw the crown on her head, they would see her as a threat, and while I was fighting him, they might attack. "We will do what we have to do. I won't let him hurt you, or anymore of your people. Jax, once we leave, make sure your men get everyone to earth as quickly as possible. They need to be protected. They will stay with them until I send someone. Make sure they know the keywords and tell them to trust no one until you hear the words." I nodded at Eli, who bowed. He was my brother, and I hated that he bowed to me, but that was how he'd always shown his loyalty. I knew he would do his job. They both would. I had absolute faith in them.

"Luka and Ryker, you're with me. We need to make it look like we have taken Freesia hostage." I looked to Luka and Ryker.

"We made these cuffs." Ryker came closer, but I saw Freesia back up a couple steps. "They aren't iron, baby girl," Ryker said. "They won't sap your power, but you need to contain it. The bad, bad King needs to think you are contained, okay?" Freesia nodded, and I relaxed. If she let Azreal know she could still do magic, it could ruin everything.

"Trust me, love. I swear I will protect you with my dying breath if I have to." I kissed her lips. I couldn't stop myself.

"Don't make that vow. Ever. Because if I live through this, I want you with me, always." She glared at me, and I nodded. I knew what she was feeling. I wanted her with me always as well.

"Okay, I will save my vow until after we beat Azreal." I grinned, but she just glared at me.

"I will never accept a vow like that from you. I want your love, not your loyalty," her voice nearly broke. "I want you, Weston. I don't want anything else. Not this crown, or to have to deal with your father. I just want us to be together."

"As soon as my father is out of the way, we can be together, just you and me." I pulled her into my arms and kissed her lips. I loved my Ice Princess more than anything, and I wouldn't let anyone threaten her. Not even my father, *especially* not my father or his minions. "I know you don't want vows, but I can't help myself." I grinned as I knelt, and both Luka and Ryker did the same.

"What are you doing?" She gasped.

"I give my life over to the Ice Queen," I said in monotone. I wanted her to know this had nothing to do with her title, but the way I felt about her. "I will give my life to you, Freesia, for eternity."

"Stop it," she exclaimed. "Are we entirely sure he doesn't know we are mated?" she screeched.

"No, we can't be sure, but you're right. I need to stop making this harder." I shook my head. "I will not make any more vows until after we have defeated Azreal. I am sorry."

"You don't need to be sorry. You just need to stay alive. I don't want to have to live the rest of my life without you," she sighed, wrapping her arms around me.

"Precious, you will never have to live without me, I can

promise you that without any kind of vow tearing us apart." I kissed her lips.

"Can you promise that?" she asked.

"Yes, baby, we are linked for eternity," I said softly. "If you die, I will follow you into the abyss. And if I die, you will follow me. But I refuse to let either of those things happen. We will come out of this alive. I will make sure of it." That seemed to appease her, and she nodded.

"Okay, let's get this over with." She looked down at Luka and Ryker, who were still kneeling. "I won't accept any crazy vows of loyalty from you two either, so you may as well get up," she snapped.

"You may not accept them, but you have them, my Queen." Luka winked, and Freesia rolled her eyes.

"You're impossible," she huffed.

"They are warriors, precious. They are showing their loyalty to their Queen. Do not mock that. When we defeat my father and you take your place as the Queen of the Ice Kingdom, you will have many warriors swearing their lives to you." I stood and pulled her into my arms. "You cannot be callous with their vows."

"Fine," she sighed. "I accept your vows. Just get up off the floor, and don't die," she grumbled, looking at Luka and Ryker.

"That we cannot promise, my Queen. We will defend you with our lives if necessary, and it may very well be." Ryker was always the more serious one. I shook my head because he wasn't making this any easier on her. I watched as she deflated a little. She had a good heart and didn't want anyone to die protecting her.

"What about the mark?" Luka smirked. "How you going to hide that?" Freesia's hand clamped over her neck as she blushed bright red. You wouldn't think someone with such luminous skin would be able to turn that color. I chuckled. She was so fucking adorable. "No need to be embarrassed, little Queen. We are all adults here." He winked at her.

"We aren't hiding. He will overlook it at first glance, but it will give me the perfect opportunity to challenge him." I said it with confidence, but if he got close enough to my mate to see the mark, then he could end the challenge before it had even begun.

"Okay, let's go then," Freesia sighed, and held out her arms for me to put the cuffs on.

"These won't hurt like the others did. There is no iron in them. They are just for show. You are in complete control here," I whispered as I snapped them around her wrists. I hated being the one to chain her, but I wouldn't let anyone else do it either. I kissed her forehead softly. "Let's go." I hoped this wouldn't prove to be a huge mistake.

21

We walked through the forest for hours to reach the castle. It was nothing like I'd expected. He'd overtaken a castle made of ice. "Do your people not feel cold either?" I asked quietly. Ryker shook his head and put a finger to his lips in warning. Right. I was supposed to be a prisoner. Prisoners weren't usually permitted to speak freely. Whatever. I kept my head held high as the men surrounded me. Weston was to my right and had a look of complete indifference on his face. It hurt, but I knew he was doing what he had to do to protect me. It was a precarious situation we were in, and everyone had to act the part, or this would end very badly.

As we walked up the path to the castle doors, two huge men stood at attention. They grinned when they saw us and opened the doors, congratulating the men on capturing me.

Weston nodded to them as we passed. He still had that look of indifference on his face. *Easy love,* he whispered into my mind.

As soon as we'd stepping inside the palace, I'd felt strange, like the ice palace was as alive as the trees and the wind had been in the forest. A sense of peace washed over me, even though this was the last thing I should be feeling when I was about to meet the monster who had slaughtered my people.

The castle is buzzing, reacting to your presence. We will need to be careful. If anything happens to you, it could all come crashing down. Weston's words in my head had my eyes widening briefly as I looked at the domed ceiling.

This is all going to work out, Weston. It has to, I sent back to him. There was no outward sign that he'd heard me, but a strong pulse of love filled our link, and I relaxed a fraction.

We came to another set of double doors, and the two guards standing there looked more like the monsters Weston had told me to expect when I got there. They both had leathery skin pulled tight over their faces and tusk-like teeth protruded from the bottoms of their mouths. They were gigantic, and their clawed hands moved to open the doors. I squared my shoulders and held my head high as Weston grabbed my arm in what was meant to be a rough grip but was gentle at the same time. This was all a part of the show. As we walked into what appeared to be a throne room, I exhaled a breath. This room was calling to me as well. No, not the room, but the throne in the center of it.

"My sons," boomed the man sitting on *my* throne. It made me irrationally angry seeing him lounging there. "I knew you would come back victorious, and you found the crown of ice. It has been missing since that wretch Hypernia hid it away from me." My three protectors put their fists over their hearts and bowed their heads as I stood defiantly.

Easy, he can't know you have your magic, precious. Not until the time is right. I reigned in my temper. Magic buzzed just beneath the surface of my skin. He'd stolen my throne, my home, and my family from me. It all made me angry. I wanted to punish him, but I had to calm myself, or this could all go terribly wrong.

Azreal walked toward me, and Weston flinched briefly. *This is it, love. Do not leave Luka's and Ryker's sides. They will protect you.*

I know. I love you, please be careful, I sighed into his mind.

I will. I love you. He stepped forward and in front of me, blocking my view of the monstrous man.

"What is the meaning of this, Weston?" He glared.

"She is mine. I will not let you hurt her." His posture was stiff as he spoke. Azreal laughed.

"When she is gone, we will get you a new toy to play with. You can have Marlene. She wants you enough to spend eighteen years in a frozen wasteland watching over the princess until the time was right. She failed, which is why she and Athos are currently residing in the dungeon." He waved Weston off, but he only moved closer to me. I didn't cower behind him. I couldn't, or there would be none in this room who had respect for me as Queen.

He batted Weston out of the way, and he reluctantly moved. Azreal looked me up and down. "Do you know why I slaughtered the Kingdoms and waged war on your people? Your mother and the other insufferable Queens thought to exile me and my people because of our nature. Something no Dark Fae can help. So, we left Avalon and formed our own society, biding our time until we were strong enough to take back our home. Now, we will finally have dominion over Avalon, once you and the other princesses are dead." He ran a finger down my cheek, and it felt oily against my skin. I couldn't flinch, though. I held my defiant glare, even as I wanted to puke all over him just from the feel of his touch alone. He moved his hand and looked down further. "It's a pity I have to kill you, you are such a pretty thing," he said absently. His gaze darkened as he grabbed my chin roughly, tilting my head to the side before whirling on Weston. "You marked her?" he roared.

"I, Weston, first son of Azreal, challenge you father for my rightful place on the throne." Weston spoke clear and strong with all the confidence I knew was inside him. As soon as the words left him, Luka and Ryker pulled me behind them, drawing their weapons. I felt Eli and Jax at my back doing the same. I hadn't even seen them when we walked in.

"What is this treachery? My sons protecting the princess who ruined us as a people." Azreal roared. He was losing his temper, and that could be extremely dangerous. Weston shrugged as he pulled an obsidian blade out of thin air.

"She is my mate. My very life, and I will protect her with my dying breath if necessary," Weston growled, widening his stance. "You must accept my challenge, father. It has to be a fair fight. If you cheat, you lose. The Gods demand it." The room pulsed with magic in that moment, as if even the walls were agreeing with Weston.

People backed away until there was a wide circle around the two men. Ryker pushed me back and out of the way, even as he kept his eyes on any possible threats to me. They were all crowded around me, not watching Weston square off against the maniacal king, but watching the crowd in case someone attacked. No one was looking my way, though. They were all transfixed on the fight getting ready to happen.

I sent all my strength and love through the link, and Weston winked from his spot across the room. "I will take no pleasure in killing you, my son, but it must be done. You linked yourself to my enemy so when I kill you, she still dies," Azreal boomed as he struck out at Weston. I gasped. I could feel frost on my fingers as the two men fought in front of me.

"Not now, my Queen," Ryker whispered. I didn't know how he knew. His eyes were still on the crowd. I calmed myself and willed the frost away. I couldn't help Weston now. All I could do was pray to the Gods that he would make it through this.

22

WESTON

He was sloppy in his anger and hatred. I didn't let myself get cocky, though. I had to stick to the plan. Wear him down until I could deliver the final blow. Everything depended on this one moment. If I lost, the entire realm would be lost, and I would not be around to defend it. I couldn't let that happen. I had been training for this for centuries.

Azreal struck, and I blocked his heavy blow easily. I could tell the more I went on the defensive, the more frustrated he was getting. We circled each other. He tried taunting me, but I was zoned in on one thing. Defeating my evil father. He slashed at me again, and I parried with a strike of my own, hitting him in his sword arm, and causing a hiss to escape him.

I heard the clash of swords on the far side of the room and glanced over to see my brothers fanned out around Freesia, each fighting their own opponent. The distraction was almost enough for Azreal to get the upper hand. Freesia screamed just in time for me to turn and block his strike that was aimed for my neck. "Too slow, old man," I taunted him. It had the desired effect, making him even angrier. He slashed wildly, and I blocked with fluid ease, getting in a couple jabs at him when he left himself open to attack.

He started to slow, and I grinned. I wasn't out of the woods yet, though, because I knew if he felt himself losing, which he clearly was, he would stoop to fighting dirty. Just as I thought it, he threw a ball of fire at me that I was able to dodge easily. It was a cheap shot using his magic. More fireballs came at me in rapid succession, and I pulled a shield from the ether and positioned it to deflect them back at him.

This was getting dangerous because we were in a damn castle made of ice. Every time a fireball hit the wall behind me, it sizzled. I needed to do something drastic, but my mind couldn't come up with anything. I clenched and unclenched the fist that wasn't holding the shield and felt something cold in my hand. I dodged another fireball and looked down to find an ice dagger in my hand. What the fuck? Not wasting any time, I threw the dagger straight for Azreal's heart. He deflected at the last second, but I was already ready with another one.

We stayed like that for a while, conjuring fire and ice, and throwing it at each other from a distance until a scream and a huge blast knocked everyone in the room to the ground. I jumped to my feet quickly, not caring about Azreal. The only one who mattered was Freesia. It had been her who'd screamed and blasted everyone to the ground.

My eyes searched for her until I saw her huddled over Ryker, sobbing. She wasn't looking around her, and I nearly lost it when I saw Azreal making his way to her. He wanted to end the challenge by ending her, which would kill me at the same time. Rage pulsed through me, and I grabbed for an obsidian dagger, and threw it as hard as I could at his back.

At the last second, one of his guards stepped in front of him, and impaled himself on the blade. Azreal turned. "That was a cheap shot, boy."

"You going after my mate to end the challenge is against the rules. So is your guard stepping in to protect you," I growled back. Freesia looked up at him. Her eyes were glassy from crying, but the absolute rage in them was what had me pausing. She was all things good and innocent in this world, but right then she looked like an avenging angel as her hands glowed with blue light.

"This ends now," she yelled. Her hands shot out and what looked like blue fire arced from her palms, wrapping around Azreal. He screamed and convulsed until there was nothing left of him but ash. She slumped to the floor next to Ryker, looking up at me with tired eyes. "Is he gonna be okay?" she asked softly. I ran over to where she was looking down at Ryker, and a soft sob left her throat. It looked like he had a nasty gash to the back of his head, but it was already starting to knit itself back together.

"He will be fine, my love. We are much harder to kill then

normal Fae. He's already healing." I wiped a tear from her cheek, and she launched herself into my arms. "I thought I was going to lose you there for a moment." I squeezed her tight. The monster was dead. Not by my hand, but it didn't matter. The rightful ruler of the ice Kingdom had taken back her throne, but we still had so much work to do. The other Kingdoms still needed to be restored. We would have to find the other lost princesses and restore the Kingdoms.

Picking her up, I walked over to the steps in front of the throne of ice and set her down gently. "Only you are meant for the throne, my love. I will be your consort for all eternity, but this is for you alone." She shook her head repeatedly.

"No, I don't want a consort. I want a king. Maybe this is a matriarchal society, but we are equals in every way. I may be ruling, but you will be by my side every step of the way." She kissed my lips, and I groaned. I wanted her now more than ever, but we still had Fae to deal with.

A smaller throne appeared next to hers, and I felt something heavy on my head. She grinned at me as I looked back at her with wide eyes. "The earth chose you as well, my king. We will rule together for eternity." She kissed my lips softly.

She broke the kiss to pull me up to the thrones. I knew nothing would ever be the same. I was the King of the Dark Fae and she was the Queen of Ice, but we would bring the worlds peace if it was the last thing we did.

When we sat on the thrones, blue light enveloped us, and everyone in the room kneeled. They knew who their loyalties were with at this point, and they would never defy us again.

23

———————

FREESIA

I had been so scared for Ryker. He'd taken a sword to the back of his head while protecting me. I'd been too slow to stop it, but just like Weston had said he would, he recovered within a day. I was so happy that none of the men had died. Luka pouted for a while because I didn't cry when his arm was severed, but he didn't almost die, he'd just lost a limb that did in fact grow back in a day as well.

"Little Queen, you wound me," he said with a wink.

"Did you look dead?" I asked with a raised brow, and he chuckled. "That's what I thought." I rolled my eyes.

Since Weston had become my king, I was able to access the link between him and his brothers, which seemed to be both a blessing and a curse because I still didn't have complete control over my thoughts and they were intrusive bastards. "Stay out of my head," I growled at him.

"Stop shouting your thoughts at me, little Queen." He grinned, and I flipped him the bird. It was a human thing I'd learned from earth, but he got the idea. He bowed his head, that ever-present smirk of his still on his face.

"Do we know yet where the other princesses are? Azreal's minions will not stop, even though I have taken my rightful throne. They need to be protected." That had been the reason for the audience to begin with, but Luka was throwing a fit because I didn't cry for his now healed limb instead. "This is crazy. Luka, you need to go and find the next princess. The vampire princess is probably in the earth realm. We need to find her before Ezekeal does. I'm sure he is already searching after news of Azreal's death. They will want to keep all the other Kingdoms themselves to wage war against us. We won't allow that to happen. We will take back the Avalon and send the rest of those demons to hell." I growled and Weston looked at me with an approving smile.

"I love you, my blood thirsty mate, but we have another reason for this audience. We have some people to try for crimes against the Queen." As Weston said the words, the double doors opened and Marlene, Athos, and Baskin were pushed inside. I glared at the prisoners but didn't show any outward sign that I gave a shit what happened to them. Athos and Baskin looked at me with apologetic eyes, while Marlene watched Weston on the throne next to mine. I stood and walked toward them. Guards followed close to me, even though the prisoners were encased in iron. I smirked.

"It hurts, doesn't it?" I asked with a raised brow. I knew

exactly how much placing someone in iron hurt. I still had scars on my wrists from my time being subjected to it. "Marlene. You can't handle the cold, can you? It's why you told me to never leave the compound. You caged me, but I won't do the same thing to you. No, I will make things much worse for you." Ice covered my hand, and I wrapped it around her throat. "You will stay encased in ice in the garden of the Snow Wolves compound for eternity. You will be forced to see life forever, but never experience it. That is your punishment for your evilness to me." All she did was glare at me as I encased her in ice. She would never hurt anyone ever again.

"Please, Freesia." Baskin looked at me with watery eyes.

"The only one who has the right to spare you or kill you, Baskin, is my king. You tried to force me from my true mate because of something that was done without my knowledge when I was an infant. It may not be your fault, but your reaction is. You tried to control me and take me from my mate. You worked with my enemy to cage me. But the worst is what you did to my mate, so he will decide your fate." I looked up at Weston. I didn't want to hurt Baskin, but I had to show strength. I had to show that I was a Queen who could rule both the ice Kingdom and the Dark Fae, even if the latter didn't want me.

Weston stepped up next to me and pulled me into his side. I knew he wanted to hand out Athos' and Baskin's punishments. I kissed his cheek.

"You can have their punishments, my king." I smiled at

him. He kissed my forehead before looking back at Baskin and Athos.

"You beg for your life?" Weston asked with an authority I had never heard from him before, but it sounded so sexy coming from his lips. They both nodded vigorously. "Then swear your lives to your King and Queen," he commanded, and I grinned. Weston was good. He was the perfect king.

They both spoke the necessary vows, and when I looked over at Luka, he was smirking as always. Ryker looked stone-faced for the most part, but I could feel his amusement through the link.

We'd removed or killed everyone we could find still loyal to Azreal, and the rest of the Dark Fae had been required to swear their allegiance to us or they would be executed. Our journey was hardly over when it came to Avalon and its problems, but we were definitely here to stay, and if anyone challenged us, we would destroy them. But first we needed to find the vampire princess.

ACKNOWLEDGMENTS

Acknowledgements
I have the best family in the world! They put up with my crap and are super supportive. Especially, my mom and sister. They are the best!
My DAT girls, you know who you are. Thank you so much for always being there for me during this crazy journey. I will always love you! (Even when you send me questionable pictures of Justin Beiber.)
All of the amazing Indie Authors and bloggers I have met over the last year! I freaking FLOVE you! You have made the last year one of the best and I can't wait for the next!

ABOUT THE AUTHOR

Ember-Raine Winters lives in sunny California with her two beautiful kids and a wolf. Also known as, Apache her pure white Siberian Husky. She loves writing romance and reading just about anything she can get her hands on. And, football! She loves watching football and going to games. It's one of her favorite ways to unwind. She dislikes the super-hot temperatures in her city and exercise. She hates to exercise but somehow her sister still gets her to do it every day. She also thinks it's completely awkward talking about herself in third person. Ember loves connecting with readers so don't be afraid to stalk her and drop her a line on social media.

 facebook.com/AuthorEmberrainewinters

 instagram.com/emberrainewinters

Addicted

Speechless (TBD)

Standalone

Christmas for the Byrds (A standalone Novella)

Fantasy Romance

Leprechaun's Kiss

Leprechaun's Mate

www.ingramcontent.com/pod-product-compliance
Lightning Source LLC
Chambersburg PA
CBHW072223150726
48002CB00005B/1938